After reading almost hundreds and hundreds of book on sci-fi and fantasy, historical novels and reference books, AW Lathan has just found out that the best book to read is the one that you write yourself. Having worked in the transport industry for many years, he thought it was about time to write a book himself which incorporates his interest in ancient and early Medievel history. He lives in darkest Somerset with his fat cat called Fluff. All illustrations in this book were drawn by the author.

Copyright © A. W. Lathan (2018)

The right of **A. W. Lathan** to be identified as author of this work has been asserted by him in accordance with section 77 and 78 of the Copyright, Designs and Patents Act 1988.

All rights reserved. No part of this publication may be reproduced, stored in a retrieval system, or transmitted in any form or by any means, electronic, mechanical, photocopying, recording, or otherwise, without the prior permission of the publishers.

Any person who commits any unauthorised act in relation to this publication may be liable to criminal prosecution and civil claims for damages.

A CIP catalogue record for this title is available from the British Library.

ISBN 9781788236966 (Paperback)
ISBN 9781788236973 (Hardback)
ISBN 9781788236980 (E-Book)
www.austinmacauley.com

First Published (2018)
Austin Macauley Publishers Ltd
25 Canada Square
Canary Wharf
London
E14 5LQ

# A. W. Lathan

# Angelina Janny Jones And The Lost Norn

Austin Macauley Publishers™
London * Cambridge * New York * Sharjah

I dedicate this book to my parents and to all the authors that have gone before me, and all authors that I have yet to read. And to the 9 year old who asked me for more monsters. and to Diane Biddulph for proof reading this book.

Marvel Graphics Novel No. 15 The Raven Baner
by Alan Zelenetz/ Charles Vess

God and Heroes from Viking Mythology
by Brain Brian Branston/ Giovanni Caselli

Every Boy and Girl a Swimmer
by W. D Dowing

A dictionary of Fairies
by Katharine Briggs

British and Irish Mythology
by John and Caitlin Matthews

## Chapter - 1
### Day - 1

# Down The Hole

Hello my name is Angelina and I am here to tell you of the fascinating and most scary and terrifying five days of my life. It all started one September morning as I awoke to the noise of my lovely dog alarm and I remembered it was the first day of the school term, so I jumped out of my bed and ran into the bathroom when I heard my mother's voice float up from the kitchen, "Angelina your new school clothes are in the airing cupboard, your breakfast is almost ready, hurry up and get dressed."

"All right mother," I shouted down the stairs as I made my way into the bathroom where I had a quick shower, cleaned my teeth and combed my long hair out and ran back into my room. After grabbing my uniform I removed the cover. Oh my God look at it, the school blazer was so bright, burgundy red or scarlet. It was hard to look at in sunlight, there was also a blue-grey knee length plaid pleated skirt, a light blue blouse, knee high black socks and one grey jumper lined in gold on the cuffs and bottom. And the good old school red and gold striped tie which had been retained for the new year. I put the blazer on the bed and pulled out my school shoes from under the bed where I had put them six weeks ago. As I stood up I could see as I glanced out of my bedroom window that out side it was a typical September day, bright and breezy. I quickly got into the uniform and ran to the bedroom door and as I opened it my hand brushed my blue holiday bag, and I remembered my holiday with my dad on the island of Malia where he has a job for six months teaching holidaymakers to dive. I had a lovely time in the Mediterranean sea, and then I remembered I had not unpacked it since I had come home last night, "oh well" I thought "I can always unpack it after school."

In the kitchen I had a good breakfast of egg on toast, fruit juice and a cup of tea to wash it down and as mother had on the radio to hear the 8 o`clock news I listened to the usual rubbish as I ate until I heard an interesting topic about some girls who had vanished from their bedrooms leaving no trace but a curious puddle of water in the middle of the floor and all the contents in the room had disappeared as well. The door and also the windows had been locked from inside the room. "Come on Angelina, eat up your breakfast. I have to go to work, I will drop you off at the bus stop on the way, and do not forget your sports bag in the hall and school book bag."

"OK mother" and I put my dishes in the sink and walked into the hall to collect my bags and coat and met my mother at the door. "Where is your new blazer," shouted my mother at the front door as she opened it up. Blazer, "Oh" I said "it's up in my room on the bed." Well go and get it now, and do not lose my old school tie," said my mother. "All right" I cried as I ran up to my room.

As I ran in the door swung closed with a thud and paying no attention to it I put on the blazer and buttoned it up as fast as I could. As I turned round I saw my reflection in the mirror on my dressing table and the sunlight shed light onto the school badge making it shine brightly, the image of St Diana holding up the sword of light and the school motto 'Truth and Justice' inscribed in gold and dark blue stood out and gleamed as did the seams on the blazer. Delighted I did a wonderwoman spin, my skirt flying around me and as I started to go to the door SPLASH. What? I looked down at my feet where my shoes and socks were in several inches of water, "Mother" I cried "I have a water leak," and as I ran to the closed

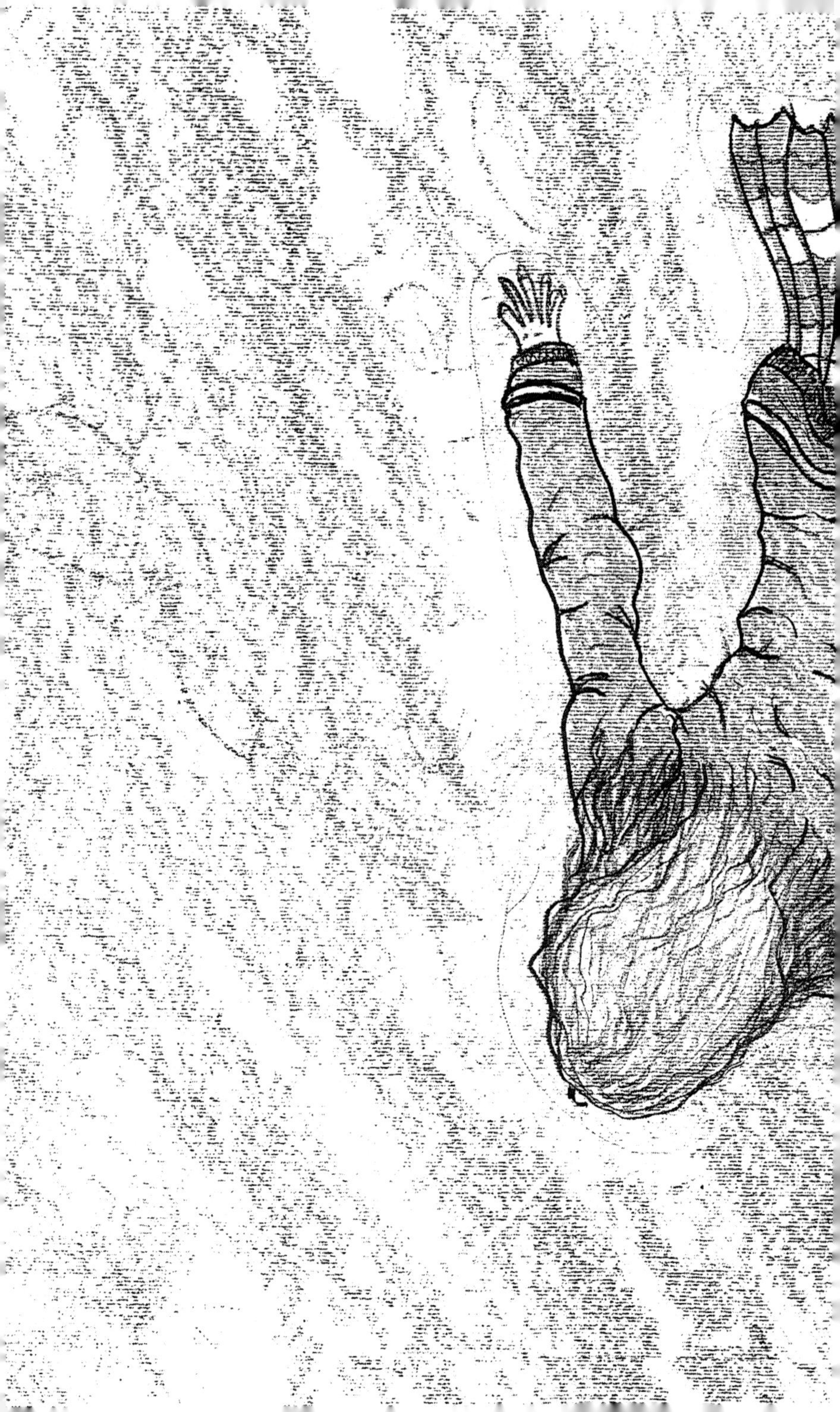

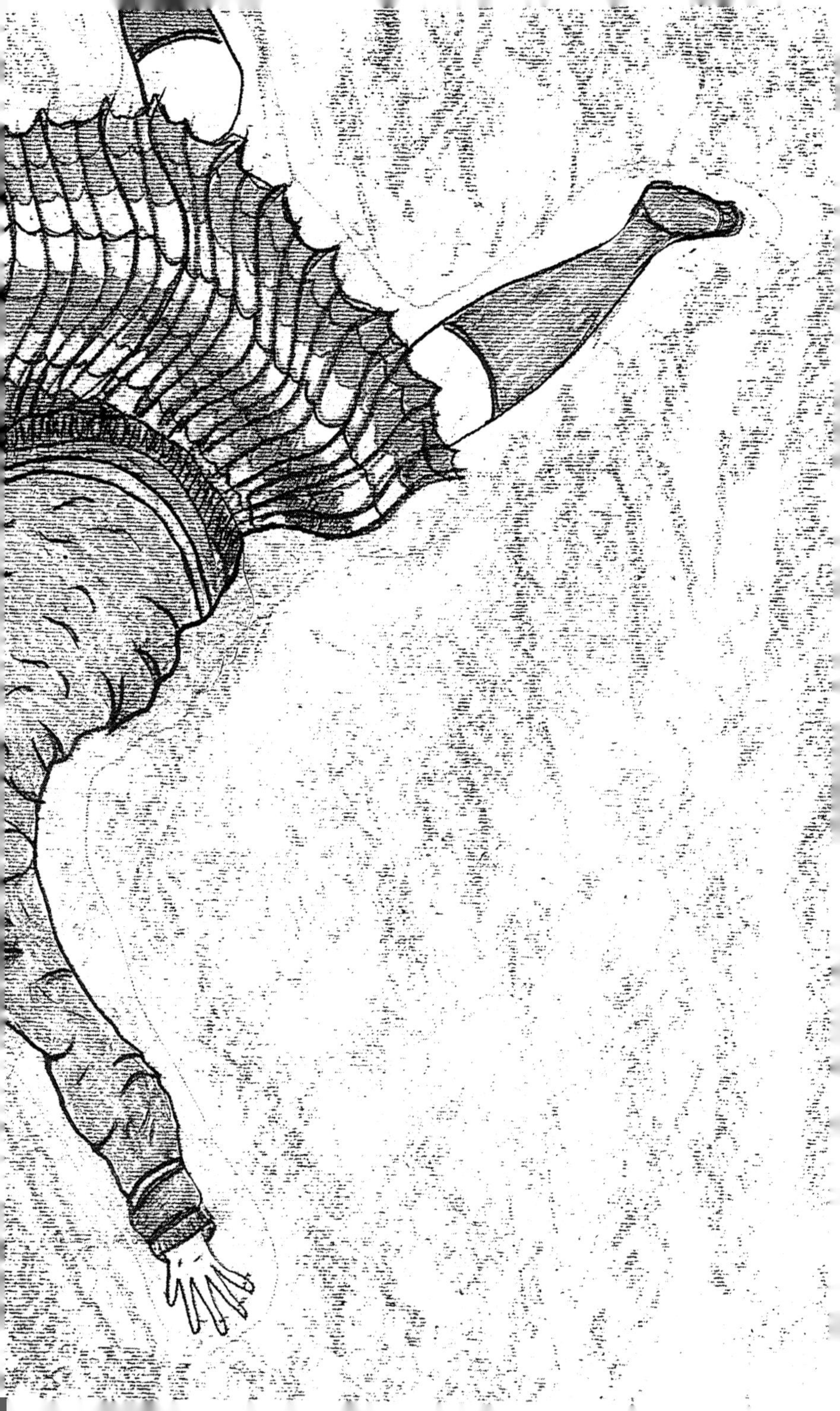

door water began to climb up to my thighs slowing me down, it was then I heard a roaring noise under my feet and all the water started to vibrate violently as it rose up to my waist, soaking my skirt and the bottom of the blazer.

It was then that the floor fell from under my feet as I leapt for the door which I missed, but fortunately my hands hit my holiday bag instead and I hung on for dear life, hoping the hook would hold, as the water appeared all around me and I managed to swing my bag about and wished I had not because in the middle of the room was a big black whirlpool on the floor, a whirling vortex of spiralling water. I looked in disbelief as all my room furniture was pulled down, my bed, carpet and the desk all vanished down into the void of darkness. As I watched in horror at what was happening I swung the bag back round and hoped the hook would hold on as I reached for the door handle and three things happened at once. The hook gave way as the door opened to reveal the terrified face of my mother, and I fell screaming into the black abyss. I fall fall fall screaming until my breath disappeared; oh no air, no air …oh my God I am going to die (BOING) then my back hit something soft and very soggy, a rubber lined tube. I could tell it was big and round as it slowed down my descent somewhat and I began to feel a forceful power on my back where I was no longer falling, but I was whirling about very fast, and I could feel my breath coming back into me, and I gulped air into my lungs at last, but I was still falling only now sideways at an alarming rate, and now I heard the sound of water below me. As I looked down I saw the big whirlpool below me, oh no. A quick deep breath and another, and then I plunged into the whirlpool, ERK. I found the water uncomfortably warm as I was dragged under into the whirling mass where I tried to kick my legs and arms but I was still holding my holiday bag in my arms.

I tried to loosen the ties around my hands, but the straps held on so tightly to my hands so I desperately reached up for the emergency red cord which was on top the bag and pulled it. And suddenly I heard a loud hiss of gas by my ear and with a WHOOSH the bag above me expanded into a two-man bright orange inflatable dinghy and together the dinghy and me shot up to the surface where I must have done a somersault at least one or two times in the air before I landed flat on my back in an upright dinghy with my bag by my legs. "Wow" I cried. I did a snow angel to stop me from falling out. As I lay in wet misery gasping for breath and grasping the sides of the dinghy, I looked up to see where I had come from, or fell down from, to see above me a long tunnel or a funnel - I could not tell which. The tunnel was all brownish in colour and very transparent and as I looked about me I could see more of them all around me. All this I took in at a glance as the dinghy and I were still in the mad whirlpool, and all I could do was close my eyes and hope for it to stop but it did not. Then I did open my eyes and saw my school tie and looked down at my new uniform. Oh my mother is going to kill me for ruining my uniform, oh well cannot be helped now just hope for the best.

I closed my eyes again as me and the dinghy were whirled about for a long, long time until I could feel the flow slowing down somewhat and, still cold and wet, I at last opened my eyes to look about me. The first thing I saw was big branches of a massive trunk from an almighty big tree, and I mean it was huge, and in between were lots of other tunnels all twisting in and out of the big looking branches. And in the branches I could see bizarre looking buildings all ship shaped and weird looking and WOW the whirling was slowing down at last and I was able to sit up and look at my surroundings. The water had stopped at last and I could see as I looked downwards into the tunnel a very big round bubble heading up to me. "Wow" I cried this time in some panic as I flopped over onto my stomach and braced my legs and arms against the sides. I closed my eyes tightly and hoped for the best. POP, the dinghy went flying up and down with me in it, the water was wild and tumbling and terror was not the word for it as I was drenched again, "Pop" and again "Pop" and "Pop." And then suddenly it stopped and I was upside down at the time holding my breath, and I was holding on to the dinghy ropes. I opened my eyes to look down and I could see the end of the tunnel opening up into darkness and then one more "Pop" and me and dinghy were sent flying out into the void.

Screaming, I must have fallen a good 20 feet when a hot wind hit my face and my wet school skirt flew up to my nose and my arms were almost pulled out of their sockets as I was thrust upwards and backwards. "Eeek" I cried and to my great amazement I looked up and now the dinghy was acting as a parachute as it was full of hot air, "Oh – whoo, this is nuts" I cried as I was flung wildly forward and backwards clinging on grimly to my dinghy ropes. It was then that I heard a big splash below me and as I looked down I could not see anything but only blackness, but I definitely heard water, oh no more water please I just hope it is warm. As I floated downwards I could manage to control my descent by pulling on the dinghy ropes somewhat, hey I could see light ahead, I could definitely see some brilliance in front and on either side of me, and then suddenly a big black column loomed up in front of me. "Eeeeek" I screeched and quick-wittedly I thrust my legs up to shove it off, but the side of the dinghy hit the column with a glancing blow that spun me about and all the lights vanished only to appear a second later.

As I spun slowly about I beheld a vast and endless forest of columns and an enormous lake all shining in greenish light. As I looked down at the water I cried out "oh no." this is going to hurt when I hit that water at my speed of descent, I would have to time it perfectly and do a dive, as down and down I went. I thought I would try a plain forward dive and hopefully it would work. And at the last moment I let go into a somersault, tucked my knees as tightly as possible then dropped head and shoulders forward before straightening out into my dive, SPLASH I hit the water in a forward header. Down and down I plunged into warm water, as I began to kick my legs for buoyancy and pushed down my skirt, I put my arms to my sides to float to the surface as old instructions forced their way into my reeling head where they echoed: "hands to your sides, do not struggle and you will rise to the surface." Those were the words my school swimming teacher had said to me, so heeding them I forced my hands to my sides and I immediately began to rise up, up to the surface, where I emerged into total stygian blackness.

I am ashamed to inform you that I panicked like a six–year old who found herself in the deep end of the pool for the first time and I must have thrashed for some time swallowing bits of warm water, sinking under for some time then floating back up, as I came up once more my wet school tie tip slapped me on my chin which brought me to my senses (calm down, calm down). I tried a horizontal float but I found that too difficult to achieve due to my wet school clothes so I began to tread water instead, and I did this for some time trying to calm myself down and recover some strength and clear my mind to think clearly. Right, first things first, off with my heavy wet uniform and as I started to pull off my blazer I suddenly thought if I lost all my clothes I would have no clothes to wear at all and I will need their warmth when I get out of this lake. Right, now where is the dinghy, so I did a spinning top to look for it and turning round I kicked my legs to the right and to the left to find the dinghy lights which would be on by now. Ah, not too far away to swim so I began to use the crawl stroke but as I began to swim the wet edges of my blazer lapels sides kept hitting my chin, so I did the breast stroke instead. Now, out of necessity I have swum in my uniform before but that was in my summer uniform in a frock when I had to rescue a girl who had fallen in the river by the head's house some two years ago, but not in full school uniform with shoes before and not in my old grey woollen blazer and it was so easy to do. I was glad I was in my pleated skirt and not in trousers and I was so happy it was not too far to swim to the dinghy, but as I got to it, it was upside down with one side still underwater as my holiday bag was pulling it down. Oh God, here I go again and I took two deep breaths and ducked underwater to find the bag to undo the clasp where I was glad to find no current to speak of, and it was no fun to feel blindly in the dark for the clasp, then my hand brushed a strap and with my fingers I grabbed the bag and released the clasp and quickly resurfaced. Now for the hard bit to right the dinghy, and I heaved my wet heavy bag over the side and pushed down onto the side and over she flopped onto my head, so I was pushed underwater again. When I resurfaced gasping for air I spat out some water and pushed wet hair out of my eyes and clung to the now upright dinghy feeling exhausted, so I turned onto my back and I kicked my legs for some buoyancy and as I did my mother's tie floated to the nose. "Bloody thing" I thought as I pushed it back down into the V of my school jumper, and, motivated by the reminder of my mother, I let out a big sigh. Right, time to get into the dinghy, this is going to be so difficult and I hooked my right leg up to the side and tried to pull myself in, and after trying for some time I pulled my wet body into the dinghy.

At last I was out of danger of drowning. I lay for some time on my back exhausted then I noticed the glow of the green luminosity had come back, "oh good" I thought as I was now beginning to get cold so I sat up and looked for my bag. I pulled it to me and opening it found it was still full of water but to my utter amazement my survival bag was still intact. Good. I tried to break the seal but my hands were too cold to open it so I put my hands into the water to warm them up, as I did I saw bubbles rising to the surface, lots of them. I took my hands out and rubbed them to dry them. Once I opened my survival bag I rummaged inside to find my waterproof torch so I could see where I was and I put in the batteries. Inside the bag were two chocolate bars and I quickly ate one for some energy. Now I was feeling better I knelt up and tried to wring out some water from my uniform and my hair, and I delved into my bag to find some hair bands, one blue and one all green and red. I put the green and red one on and I fixed my torch on using a loop in the hair band and put it on top of my hair and turned on the torch and I could see a lot better.

It was then I heard something to my right, a bubbling noise, and as I turned to look at it my torch light revealed a horrible sight - it was a big shaggy head of a black-nosed animal with white eyes and big teeth in its big mouth. I screamed, it screamed and it covered its eyes with its big hairy paws and disappeared underwater and in my panic I fell onto my front and thrust my arms into the water to escape the hideous horrid thing and, terrorized, I did not stop until a wall of wood loomed up before me all of a sudden and my light revealed a big shelf which I pulled myself onto and pulled up the dinghy on to the dry self where I sat and fainted.

## Chapter - 2
### Day - 1

# Exploring

I woke up in agony as all my muscles were in pain and it was an effort to sit up. I groaned before deciding to lie motionless instead and after some time I could tell I was beginning to feel a bit better. I needed to move, so I started to do my exercises to warm myself up and after a while I managed to peel off my wet blazer and kicked off my shoes. I rolled over to the side of the shelf to rinse my hands and face in the warm water, as I was still very cold I put my hands in the water and thought just hold on one minute, safety first - I know that warm water was what I needed most but the image of the monster thing I had seen still haunted my memory as I pulled off my wet socks. I pulled my bag to me to find my blow up lifebelt and began to inflate it, put it on and fastened it up and lit the torch, so I could scan the lake or sea for any monstrous aquatic creatures that may be out there, but not a thing was to be seen.

So I looked down in the water by the side of the shelf. I saw lots and lots of fish all pink with white eyes all feeding on some green plants and algae growing just under the waterline, harmless I hoped, so I lowered my cold body into the warm water and as my school clothes were still wet it did not matter to me so much. That was lots better so I swam, I did the back crawl out into the lake, it was easier without my blazer and shoes, and I swam up and down to loosen my sore muscles up and changed into breast stroke up and down for five minutes and then trod water for a bit. I pulled myself out and sat on the edge. There I sat with my legs in the water to see what the fish would do. "Ouch! You little sods" I cried as one bit my big toe and as I pulled out my feet "little freaks" as I rubbed my toe. Oh well, on with my exercises and for the next ten minutes I rolled about on the shelf until I was out of breath that done I squeezed water out of my socks and poured water out of my shoes and put them in my bag, then I put on the blazer for warmth as it was not so wet by now, and I put the lifebelt into the dinghy. I sat in the dinghy and ate some Kendal mint cake my dad had got me up in Windermere as it was in the survival kit, and I began to plan how to get myself out of here, if I knew where here was. I put the dinghy back into the lake and put the bag at the back where I tied it up and got in and lay on my belly. I put my arms out over the sides and paddled off as no hope of rescue was possible down here and I had to find my way home somehow, so I set off to explore for some way out of this strange water world.

I followed the shelf but it soon ended, so on I paddled for a good hour or more only to find more columns all glowing in iridescent shades of greenish light under the roof of this big underground chamber. I was still scanning the waters for any encroaching things ahead of me to beware of, but all I noticed were lots of wood all floating by in long drifts, so I followed them and after a while I could hear the musical sound of a waterfall some distance ahead in the darkness and as I was so thirsty I hoped I would find some water to drink as the lake water was too salty to drink for my taste. So I paddled on a bit farther and the waterfall came into view. WOW, it was a very big waterfall, it must be half a mile wide at least, it was so dazzling as it was all lit up in green light. To the side of the waterfall was somewhat of a bay all clogged up with bits of wood and, to my alarm, as I got nearer I saw notable bits of furniture – tables, beds, bits of bookcases, toys, cupboards, chairs, trunks, boxes, dolls, books and some kind of couches and all in shreds and pieces. Oh my, I needed to see if I could utilize some of it. I saw a gap in between this pile of rubbish and the waterfall where I had to push bits of wood out of my way, but at last I managed to reach a ledge I could see where I jumped into the shallows and pulled up the dinghy to the ledge.

As I stood up my bare feet felt wood, I looked down at the ground. The whole ledge I was stood on was made out of dark wood as was all the construction of the walls all the way up as far as my torch light would penetrate, it was so weird. I turned my attention to a mass of rubbish to see what I could find. The first thing I saw was a curtain pole about six feet long, still in good shape with rotten curtains all in tatters. I undid the ties and with the pole I began searching for something useful and I began to push bits of wood out of the way to where I found a pack of briefs, a pack of black tights and lots of old school clothes in tatters and two waste paper bins that were all a bit dented. I looked up and spotted a beautiful sight, but in order to get it I had to wade out up to my waist but it was worth getting my blazer wet again as I received my gift from the pile of rubbish. It was the best weapon any schoolgirl could have for defence - a good old rounders baton! It even had a leather strap on top. I did not know at the time that this baton would save my life in the most splendid way, and now armed to face anything in case I saw any more underwater creatures, and still up to my waist in water, I began to search for any wood that could be used for kindling to make a fire to dry my soggy uniform.

I began to throw all the things I had collected onto the shelf and waded back then I saw two plastic bottles that were still in good shape, ah very handy, now I can keep some water I can hopefully drink. Back on the shelf I put on my shoes and socks and began to sort out the dry wood from my pile of flotsam to break up into a goodly pile with which to start a fire. I looked about as I needed to find somewhere to camp, but where I looked was at the waterfall and maybe there were some caves to hide in I hoped. I picked up the dinghy and took out my bag and lifted dinghy over my head, picked up one of the bottles. I waded into the splashing waterfall, and forced my way into the cascade to the other side, and I was rewarded by a large overrun cavern full of dripping water as only my feet got wet, so keeping the dinghy above my head I began to look for somewhere to hide. My torch light lit up a very big cave at the back and several holes which were too small for me to hide in, so as I moved into this roaring cave a hole appeared at the far back that by the look of it was very dry. I crouched down to the ground and crawled in, ah, good, it was nice and dry, so I crawled along to see if this hole was any good to find that it opened up into a big round bowl of a room with a hole in the roof. Ah, this will do nicely.

Back out I began to fetch and bring all the things I had found into my hidey-hole using the dinghy to keep it all dry. Right first thing first. I need food and fresh water, and with this in mind I crawled back out with the bottles and held one into the flow to clean out the dirt inside. Now for the test as I cupped my hand and I held it to my lips. Mmm, not too bad, good and fresh, now I needed something to eat as I had only had some bars of chocolate and some mint cake. I crawled back in, pulled off my blazer and hung it up over the hole opening, found my bag and opened up my survival bag to see what was inside as I had not seen in it or sorted it for sometime. Out came the Kendall cake, almost all gone, then one chocolate bar, first aid kit and a set of ten green glow sticks. I put up four of them in the roof in the tangling roots where they glowed nicely. Seeing that the hole was well illuminated now, I turned off my torch saving the batteries. Out next was a sealed tin containing six tubes of flares - 3 red and 3 white, some fire lighters, candles, a pen knife, fish hooks and line, 4 sachets of cup-a-soups and a small box of matches. But best of all there was a tin foil survival blanket, salt, tea, pepper, sugar - all in small packs as well a set of knives and forks with a handle for the tin.

The light from the glow sticks revealed a hole in the centre of the bowl I was in so I put the two tins into the hole so I could make a fire out of all the wood and piled it all around the tins in the hope they would dry. I lit one of the candles and got it going and I began to drip hot wax on the soggy wood to dry faster, soon I had a good fire going to keep me warm and dry as I opened all the packs to see if any of the tights or briefs would fit me. I put the pole into the roof and hung it all up to dry, by now the water had boiled and I had the first tin of tea with two sugars, ahh, so nice, as I sat with the survival blanket all around me. Bit by bit I fed the fire until all was dry on the pole then I stripped off my wet uniform and hung it all along the pole to hopefully dry, tried on the tights and briefs then made some soup, and as it had been such a tiring day I wrapped myself in my survival blanket and went to sleep.

# Chapter - 3
## Day - 2

# The Lake Dreaming

I had a dream that I had fallen down a very wet pipe into a dark lake and I had to swim out of it to escape all the monsters. I awoke with a start, oh, it was not a dream, but it was all too true, oh well get up, so I rolled out and crouched down by the fire to get it going again. After a bit it was burning well so I added more wood to dry on the side. That done I dug into my bag to see if I had a hair comb at all in the side pocket. Oh, good fortune it was at the bottom, so I sat down and combed out my hair and wondered what to do next as the light played over my bare arms revealing lots of bruises, all up my arms and my legs as well as I lifted my t-shirt I saw my body was all black and blue, oh my God what a sight. About time for some breakfast. I remembered seeing a gap in the waterfall, there may be some fish to catch. So on with my still-soggy shoes and now-dry skirt and blazer, and with my fish hooks, I pushed the dinghy before me out into the overhang, pulled the dinghy over my head and stepped out in the darkness then I turned on the torch to search for anything out in the darkness, but there was nothing to see. Good, so holding the dinghy over my head so as not to get too wet from the spraying waterfall, I stepped out.

After a bit I came to the end of the waterfall, pushing on I reached the side of the wall where I managed to scramble past the liquid out into a opening where a big cove was revealed where I sat down on a bit of dry wood and put the dinghy in the water, and climbed in and spinning about I pushed off into deeper water. As I looked down I thought "oh my God, look at all those fish." There was little ones and big ones all feeding on green weeds, so I pulled some up and baited the hooks with the weed and I hoped for a bite. And in no more then twenty minutes I had six fish hooked for my breakfast. I paddled back to the side, got out pulled out my dinghy and worked my way back with my catch into the bowl where I cooked all the fish and ate two hoping they were not at all poisonous - too late now. Oh well lets move on, so I wrapped up the four fish into a bag, and collected all my food, water and my gear and, putting it all into my bag, put out the fire. Now I had to put on my now dry uniform it being now a bit smelly from all the smoke and salty hot water, then I looked at my mother's old school tie, now what do I do with it? If I lost it I would not hear the last of it. So I put it on for safe keeping, so as not to lose it, then it was time to pull down the pole and then I crawled out into the overhang, pulled my dinghy over my head and waded out into what I had called Flotsam Bay where I strapped down all I had found, pulled my hair into a ponytail and I fastened my life jacket over my blazer (which was a bit of a squeeze but I succeeded). Next I needed a bit of wood to go on top of the dinghy so I can have a good vantage point to see better so I could use the pole as a paddle. Looking about I found one not too big but strong enough to lay on top of the dinghy, so I pushed out the dinghy and waded up to my knees and climbed in and paddled out into the lake keeping well out of the spray of the waterfall.

    I paddled out into darkness of this vast cavern and as I looked back at the waterfall I thought that all that water has to go somewhere so all I had to do was find it first, so on I paddled for a good two hours or more keeping the wall of wood on my left hand side. Up above in the greenish light the cavern roof was lower then before and I also noticed that the columns were somewhat shorter and up in the roof big patches of the greenish light were missing, very strange but there may be a way out at last, so I continued on my way, then KERSPLOSH something big hit the water in front of me spraying me with lots of water and almost capsizing the dinghy.

* * * *

I fell off my seat with my legs in the air and as I looked up I saw movement and I stared in shock and disbelief for in front of me wrapping itself around a column was the biggest most monstrous creature I had ever seen in my life. As I lay in complete fear the big creature revealed itself to be a large weird-looking worm of some sort sliding up the column, at this point I screamed in some fear as it had stopped moving and out of the darkness before me loomed a very large big hideous head of a lizard with big fangs with dark wood in its jaws and with big horns and cold dark eyes which looked into my eyes for an instant, went "haassshh" at me and it disappeared into darkness. I lay in the dinghy on my back transfixed in fear for some time until something hit the dinghy on the side and bounced off, and as I sat up to see what it was a big piece of wood hit the water on my left side splashing me with water, God I am being bombed by pieces of wood and I knelt down and began to paddle like mad to put some distance between me and that monster. I went back the way I had come from very, very fast and then as I paddled away I felt hot water running down my leg, oh God I must have pee'd myself in fright, adding to the water at the bottom of dinghy that sloshed about soaking my legs and the bottom of my skirt, so I had to sit back onto the plank and I zigzagged my way out into the middle of the lake. What in God's name was that thing? I can only hope that it must have been a hallucination of some kind and I pushed on into the dark, then a wall of wood loomed up on left side.

Hey I must have come to the other side at last, so I stopped my panic and followed the wall of dark wood for a hour or more. I heard the sound of gurgling water up ahead of me. At last a way out, and SPLASH a cataract of water fell down into the lake from the roof not too far away from me and as I watched lots of bits of rubbish fell tumbling down into the lake. My God all that water came down from the ceiling, I cannot be too far from where I must have fallen down into this mad under water world, so on I paddled to the side. Suddenly I saw some movement on the side and I spotted lots of dark shaggy strange-looking bodies all swimming in and out of the rubbish. Abruptly the cascade of water ceased flowing and I saw something or someone in a silver cat-suit plummet into the same spot as all the shaggy bodies. As one all the shaggy bodies dived into the depths and then all disappeared at once, only to surface dragging something away at some speed, and quickly I began to follow them to see where they had gone in the hope of rescuing whomever it was who had the misfortune to fall into the lake.

As I made my way towards the shaggy bodies, the dinghy began to bump into lots of pieces of white plastic panels with strange looking words and even half a desk of some kind with lots of colourful wires all trailing in its wake, all of which I had to push away with the pole to follow the shaggy. Mmm, that's a nice name for them. Now all this rubbish was stopping me from getting any nearer to my goal, till finally clearing all the plastic bits and pieces aside I could see up ahead in the greenish light some large Shaggy bodies which all stood together in a group next to a dark cave opening - maybe a way out. Oh God these creatures give me the heebie-jeebies. So I pulled my bag over to me to find one of my flares and gripped my rounders baton for safety, now I know the Shaggy creatures did not like bright light after my last inhabitant meeting, so be brave

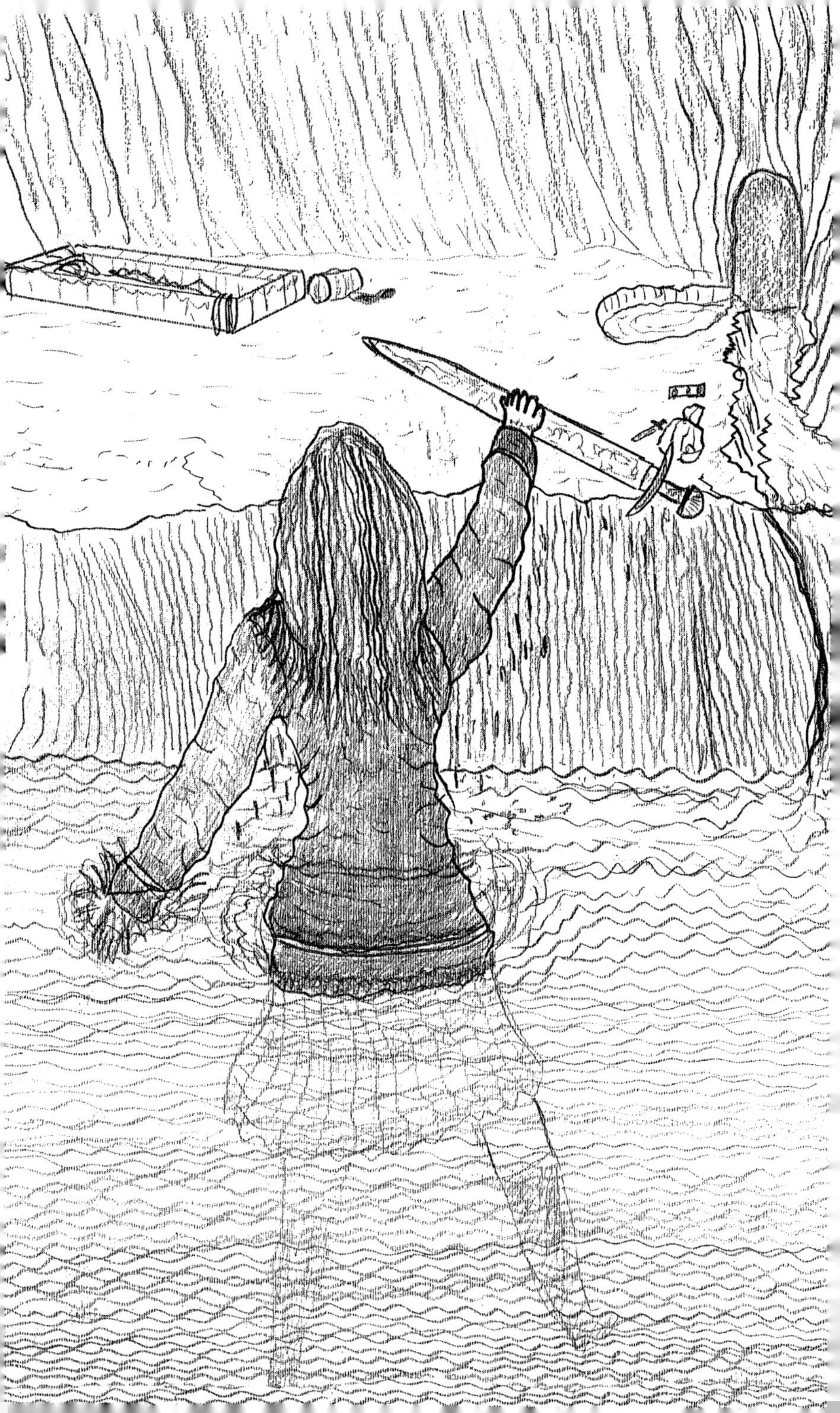

and go for it. Holding up the flare at arms length I closed my eyes and pulled the ring-pull BANG whoo. I felt heat on my head for an instant as the flare fired away and I opened my eyes to see the wonderful site of a white flare arching into the roof of this cavern. GLORIOUS. The screams and howls were great to hear, as I began to paddle very fast to the cave opening where I was glad to see lots of panicked splashing, as all the Shaggy dove into the depths.

At last I reached the cave only to find something so astonishing - a big iron griddle that was saddling the edge of a large sink hole. This was the first iron I had seen in this mad world, as I grasped the side I rolled out of the dinghy and knelt down to pull the dinghy over the lip where I did a two powerful haul up and my wet shoes slipped on the wet iron edge and I landed on top of the dinghy breaking the wooden seat, as me and the dinghy plummeted down face first into the sink hole, "Weee" I screamed.

\* \* \* \*

The first thing to happen was I had a face-full of water as the dinghy hit the flow of water in a round hole, my pole fell over the side and I shot at high speed into a low-roofed wide chamber with two openings. Which one, left or right? Left, left as I thrust my hands over the side into the water up to the cuffs of my blazer into the flow and pushed the dinghy to the left one, but before I disappeared down this hole I saw my pole shoot down the right one, oh no I lost it. This water was very swift and I had to keep my head down and hope I had chosen the right hole, this carried on for some time until over the roar of water I heard a waterfall (oh no, not again) as me and the dinghy parted company, head first I plummeted down into the roaring cascade with no time to take a breath. (ugh water up my nose). As I was spinning and whirling about my lifejacket did its job and, kicking my legs wildly, I managed to swim up to the surface out into darkness again, "do not panic" I thought my torch must have fallen off somewhere as I felt my head, so treading water I began to look underwater for it.

Ah ha it was just below me rolling away on the bottom and I must get it. So I began to untie the ties of my lifejacket, not as difficult as putting it on, and pushing it to one side began to swim over to the spot below me, took some deep breaths and then I duck-dived down, my legs in the air, down into the depths. Now this was not too easy in one's soggy wet uniform and school shoes as I had to do the breast stroke and kicking my legs I managed to swim down to grasp it, as I held it up the light lit up a hideous sight. WOW I mouthed nearly losing my breath in shock as I saw lots of bones and skulls all big and small ones in a large pile. Up, up pushing off the bottom struggling to swim in the strong side current, breaking the surface I was shivering in fear (I do so dislike skulls and skeletons). I began to swim the crawl stroke in panic, when suddenly I hit my head on my rounders baton arghh, so I had to stop my swim and grasping it I pushed it down into my blazer, and now treading water again I began to search for my dinghy or lifejacket, ah, I see it glowing red in the torch light and back into my crawl stroke I swam to it and held on to for some buoyancy and began to look for the dinghy.

Ah, there it was drifting into a round tunnel and now in no danger of drowning I began to look to see where I had ended up. I saw three openings - two small and one big - and the dinghy had gone into the farthest away, (it would be) so kicking my legs holding on to the lifejacket I swam over to the one I had seen the dinghy go into. As I swam into its opening my shoes hit bottom (ah good) and as I stood up the water was only thigh deep just below my blazer's sides, then

I saw a long tunnel ahead of me. Quickly I waded up to my dinghy, dumped my lifejacket inside where I saw my bag was in good shape as I pulled out my baton and put that in the dinghy as well. All good now let's move and see where this tunnel leads to, the Shaggy may be after me anyway. It was good to walk for once, or wade, as I know it would keep me warm after all that cold swimming I had to do, so towing the dinghy and sloshing up the tunnel I noticed in the torch light that the walls were perfectly round and very wide. The flow of the water was a bit sluggish and not too warm as I walked on for some time, then I heard the gush of water, and as I moved on slowly I saw in the torch light a small waterfall flowing into a dark lake, and a big looking cavern, (oh no is this a dead end?), and at once I burst into tears and I cried for some time.

Drying my eyes I looked all about me, on one side was a small pool next to a dry ledge. I waded over, pushed the dinghy up and over, crawled out upon to the ledge and sat down in despair. After some time I began to get cold and with no hope of a fire here I stripped off my soaking wet uniform and shoes and stockings, and I squeezed all the water out as best as possible, now I remembered the school outfitters telling my mother in the shop "school clothes are meant to keep the child warm if it gets wet." Well I would put that theory to the test, but first I dug into my bag to find my dry socks and briefs, the only dry things I had on me. Now putting on damp and cold clothes is not easy at all but in the end I managed it and feeling quite miserable I did my exercises to warm myself up. Now for some food so I ate two fish that I had left and had some water to drink, rolled up my blazer to use as a pillow, put my school shoes upside down to dry and I washed out my dirty under things, wrapped myself in my survival blanket and lay down in the dinghy and cried myself to sleep.

# Chapter - 4
## Day - 3

# Tam Lin

I was asleep for some time until suddenly I woke up with a start to the sound of someone or something splashing water up the tunnel making lots of noise. I sat up and listened carefully to it, I rolled out of the dinghy and picked up my baton and began to look for somewhere to hide. Oh, where can I hide – in the dark lake (no). The pool (yes). Quickly I submersed myself into the chilly water shuddering in the coldness. I turned off the torch which I had left on and sunk up to my nose when I had to push my floating skirt down and watched the entrance for it to emerge, hand on my baton and torch ready to leap out. A darker shape appeared swimming in and I watched as it stood up to sniff the air and as it turned towards me I turned the torch on and I rose out of the pool giving my best girlie Amazon war cry and swung my baton at it but I missed it completely and in my swinging about I lost my balance and I fell head first in to the pool with a big SPLASH, but as I hit the water there was a very bright flash of light and a screech and a thud from the creature. I came up sputtering and shaking water from my eyes and hair only to see a Shaggy by the wall of wood and very slowly it slid down the wall leaving a bloody stain and began to float toward the dark lake.

I splashed out quickly to see what the Shaggy looked like - oh my God what is it? I looked in disbelief – it was an otter, a man-sized otter, so very odd, in clothes wearing a jacket and trousers and even a belt (very weird). Gingerly I plucked the belt off the body and gave a quick look inside "gah what a smell" I cried. There was a bag of very smelly fish, oh and a small knife, oh very useful and I put the bag on the ledge and gave the body a kick over the lip of the small waterfall. I watched it sink into darkness. I waded back to the ledge and sat down my legs still in the water and I started to shake in fear as to what I might encounter next, as I looked down at myself at my now wet school clothes. Oh well, I might as well not try to keep my uniform dry as I put my mother's school tie back down into my wet school jumper (as it keeps getting out). I sat in misery thinking of some breakfast and as I stood up a bright light appeared out over the lake, as I turned and looked at it, it got brighter and out of the darkness a glowing tree appeared on an island out in the lake.

\* \* \* \*

It was then I heard the most beautiful strange song that I had ever heard in my short life. It was then my feet started to go up and down and into an Irish jig, my legs started to kick the water and dance, leap, skip and jump to the song, and I was powerless to stop my dance, as this dance took me to the edge of the dark lake and with one skip and jump I was in SPLASH. Did I stop my dance? No, instead I started to swim the butterfly breast stroke then the back crawl into the propeller then the torpedo and backward somersault leaping and larking about. Now all this swimming took me to the edge of the island in record time, then my toes hit ground and I rose out of the lake and began to dance to the song right up to the glowing tree where the song stopped abruptly, and I crashed to the ground exhausted in a soggy heap. As I lay shivering I heard laughter from above me and I looked up in some anger to see the most extraordinary unbelievable sight I have seen in this mad underground water world. For above me was a man who was entombed in the glowing tree. Only his body, one arm and leg and head was showing with long fair hair, handsome face and very muscular torso all in strange queer armour and horned helm.

The laugher stopped and he shouted at me in a language I did not understand, then he waved his arm and I saw to my horror the tree begin to move its branches towards me and I tried to move my wet cold body but it was useless. The branches began wrapping around my waist and I was lifted high into the air, the branches squeezing me so cruelly up to his face where he began to laugh at my face as I was in pain – then he stopped laughing, looked puzzled for some time, then the pain stopped and I was able to catch my breath. Then his hand gripped my wet school jumper on the left side and he looked at the school badge of St. Diana for ten seconds then let go. I was at this point weak-kneed in terror as I hung in the grip of the branches dripping water and shaking, and then I was pulled high over his head where I hung for some seconds then back down to see this man with a big smile on his face when he spoke to me in the language as before. And I shouted at him "I do not understand you" in anger, he looked at me and a look of annoyance crossed his face and then I was dragged face to face with him. He closed his eyes opened his mouth and this pink-blue mist issued from his mouth into my mouth. I tried to turn my mouth to the side but he held my chin tightly and my body jerked in spasm and I shuddered in some convulsion as I did a silent cry and it felt as if a hundred bees had stung me at once, it was then I heard a voice in my head "sleep mortal."

\* \* \* \*

When I opened my eyes I found myself lying down on my side on soft level branches and I felt so good as I had no pain anywhere, oh wow. As I sat up I noticed I was no longer wet at all and I looked

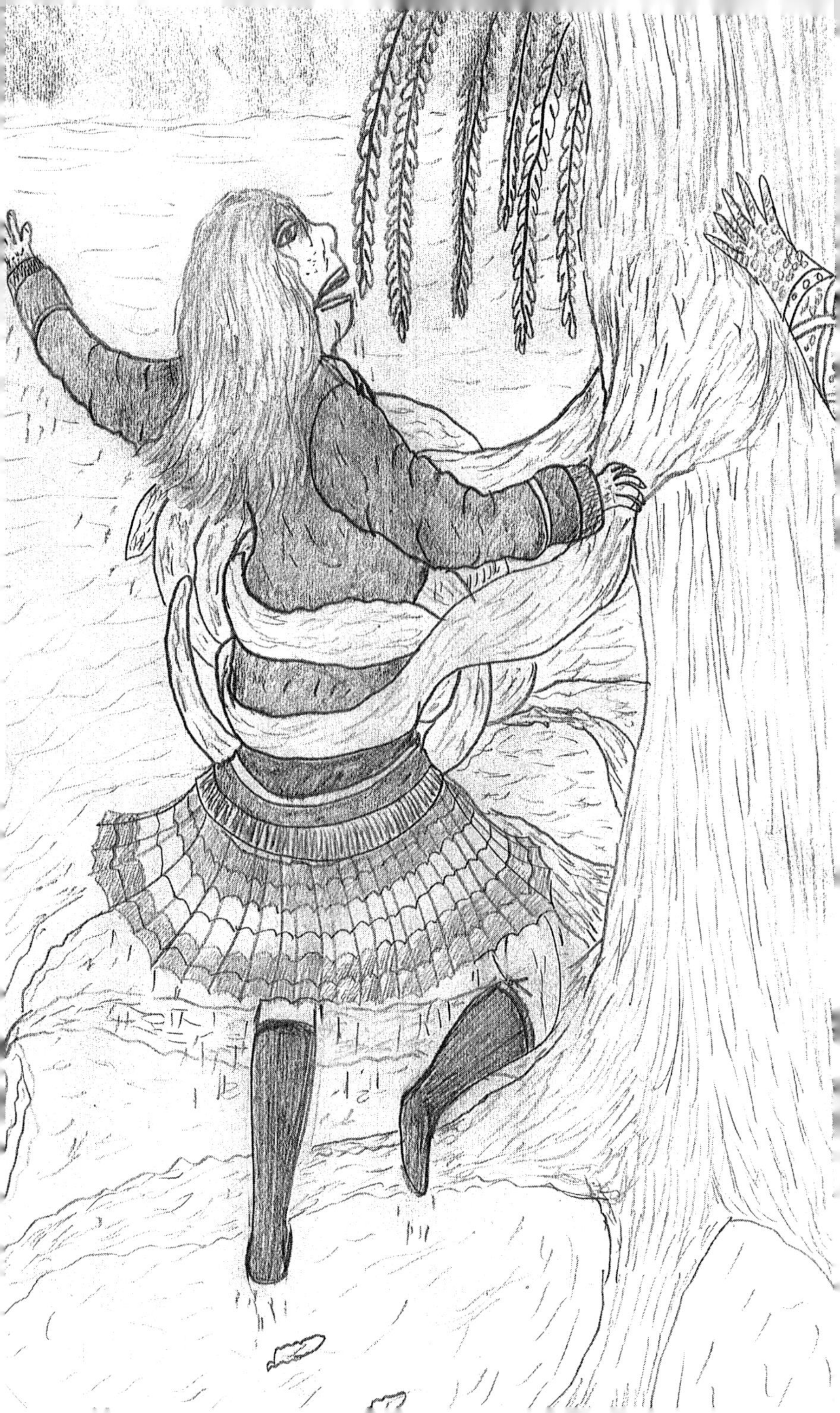

down at my uniform to see it was now all dry and as new, no tears or creases, as I put my legs to the side I saw that even the pleats of my school skirt were in straight lines and my hair was too. Oh, as I looked up the branches all moved up till I was level with the man in the glowing tree. "Greetings mortal child," in a voice I could understand at last. "Awake at last I see, good." I glared at this man in the tree in some anger. "You are a maiden-born child."

"What do who mean by mortal?" I ask. "You are my salvation child." What? "My queen has answered my plea. Who are you?" Who am I? I asked. "Yes, who are you, you are not one of the Norns creatures." What do you mean by that? "How did you escape the water trap child?"

"Heh I swam out in my dinghy."

"Dinghy? What is a dinghy?"

"My small boat." He then laughed - lots. "Tell me who you are again?"

"You first, there is power in names child."

"Oh, all right my name is Angelina, Angelina Janny Jones of 34 Dunvant Road, Swansea, Wales" I rattled off automatically.

"A powerful name you give me freely mortal, so my name is Tam Lin of the Unseelie Court, I am the guardian of Carterhaugh Wood in Carterthaugh in the north country in the kingdom of the mighty and you mortal child are so fortunate not to be Carterhaugh Wood this day for my queen has cursed me to exact a pledge from maidens who visit my well of roses, their maiden hood. But as you can see I am not in any perfection to harm you mortal child."

"Oh my God you are Tam Lin!"

"Yes mortal child."

"Oh my mother has a book of ballads and a book all about you, she can sing the ballad all the way to the end." The look of joy was wonderful to see on his face so extraordinary. "Sing it mortal child."

"What now?"

"Yes, mortal child."

"But, but." Just then all the branches dropped me to the ground where I was made to sit down crossed legged in front of the tree, I looked up at him and began to sing the ballad of Tam Lin in my best assembly hall voice. "Janet has kilted her green kirtle a little aboon her knee and she has broded her yellow hair a little above her bree and she's away to Catershaugh as fast as she can hie." It took me a good five minutes to sing the ballad all the way through to the end. "Awake, mortal child." "Huh what am I doing sat down I thought" as I jumped up to look at him in the tree. "You sing beautifully mortal child." I did blush red in the face.

"You must by hungry and thirsty child".

"Oh yes please" I replied suddenly feeling ravenous. "Here partake of this food and drink" and out of nowhere on branches appeared a bowl of food and a cup of wood. "Eat and drink child."

"Please stop calling me child. I was 14 last month" I replied as I ate and sipped from the cup which was full to the brim with something very nice and warm that tasted like honey mead, very very nice... mmm. "How is it possible for the tree to make the food and drink?" I asked him. "The tree is part of the tree of life mortal, the roots give me life, everlasting long life, it was how I healed you of all disease and injury and dried all on you."

"Oh, wow, are you saying this tree is magic?"

"No, mortal."

"Will you stop calling me mortal as well?"

"But you are mortal and now as you have food and drink of the faerie you hereafter obey me."

"What, you enchanted me? Why?"

"To finish my great task mortal." In anger now I shouted up to him, "why me?" I had had it up to here in this stupid world, I had been half-drowned and scared half to death, seen hideous looking monsters, horrifying looking big otters and a giant lizard, which gave me the willies I can tell you and fallen down a long wet tunnel. "I have had it up to here and I want to go home now pleaseee." And sobbing and crying I collapsed to the floor.

"You saw the dragon Nithog, the dread biter has terrible jaws – pierce and injure Yggdrasills roots, indeed you and me are in Niflheim at the bottom of Yggdrasill the world ash tree mortal, the realm of mist and fog the third root of the rooty bower the Norse Hel."

"What, where, how," as I looked up at him. "Yes you are the one who can free me from this long task, mortal."

"How can I do it?" I asked still sobbing. "You are blessed by the goddess Diana and under her protection mortal."

"Huh, but there is only one God, St. Diana is just my school name."

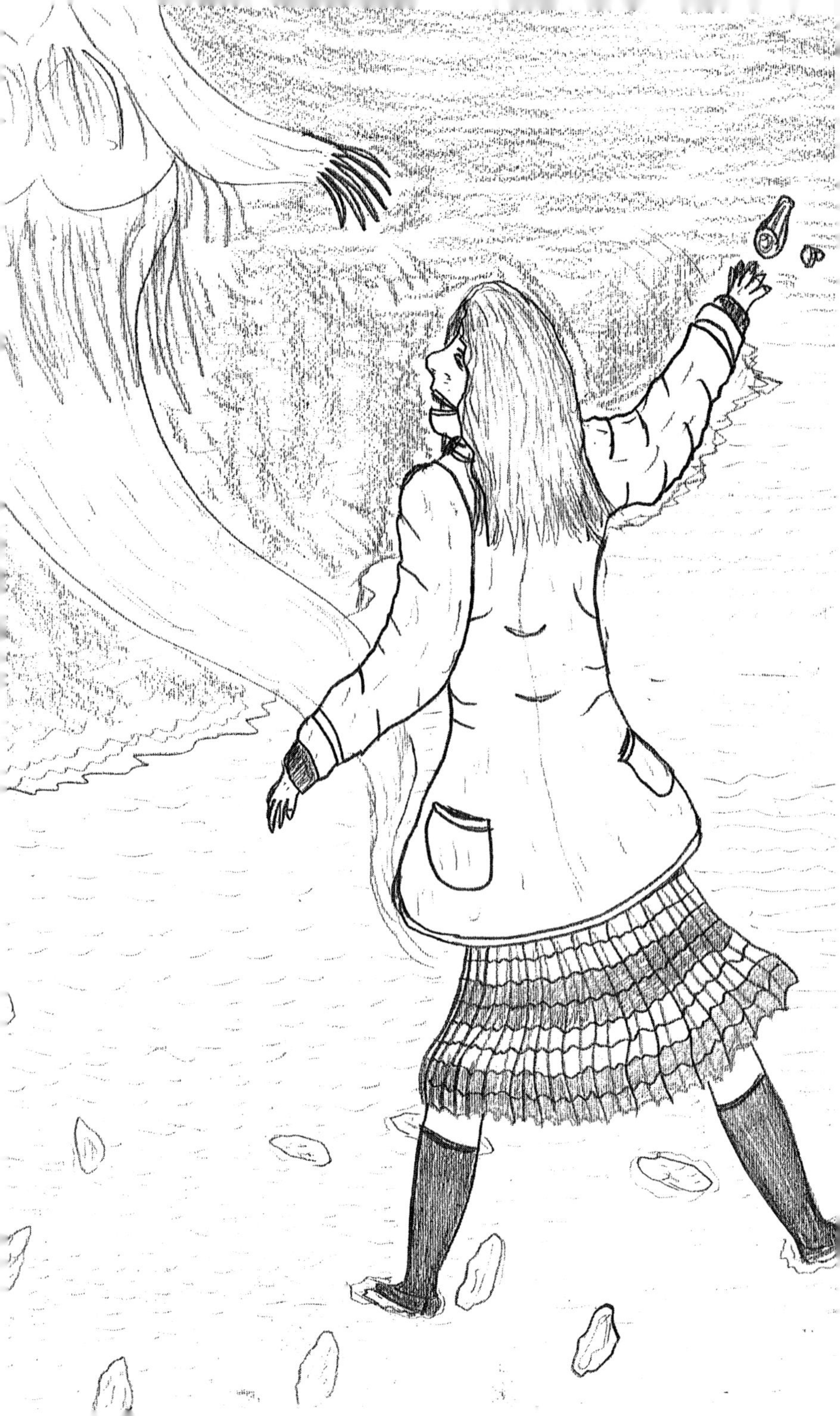

"School, what is a school?"

"It is a place for learning and for scholarships."

"Ah, you mean schole, yes it is Greek for leisure. I was schooled by a pious slave who worshipped the one god who my lord seized hold of, he give me lessons in Greek and Roman Latin."

"Ah, but slavery was abolished in the 1800th A.D. I did an essay on it at school."

"You saying I've been down here that long mortal? Gods. Drying my eyes, "yes you must have, and what is this task you want me to do?"

"You must slay the Norn at the well of Wyrd, the well of time is the only way of escape for you mortal."

"You want me to kill someone?

No mortal, you have to cut the link to the well, not kill but restore the balance, for the Norn has some of my Queen Meghens, oh to you, virgins. It was my task to stop the Norn."

"What is a Norn please and what has virgins got to do with it?"

"MORTAL, you have not been listening have you? The tunnel you fell down was to have you captured and sacrificed for the soul in you."

"What, but but ...that's evil."

"Yes but what I have to do in my wood is evil as well, but evil can do good sometimes for its own ends, and you being a powerful virgin can do what I cannot do."

"How?"

"I have two powerful artefacts for you to use."

"Huh, what is an artefact please?"

"Oh gods, do they not teach you anything at this school of yours?"

"Yes but I have not heard of artefacts before now."

"Artefacts are powerful items made by the gods and not to be used by mere mortals, but you girl are special as you have the sign of the goddess Diana on your grey vestment."

"On my what vestment? What is a vestment?"

"Pah, on your grey top mortal."

"Oh you mean my grey school jumper?"

"Yes." I see now. "Now mortal you must climb up to me, and feel down my back for Caledfwich, one of the artefacts I have for you."

"Okay, give me a hoist up please."

"If I must girl. Put your foot into my hand."

So climbing up on top of him I looked for this Caledfwich, but all I could see was a handle or hilt, so grasping the hilt I pulled it out to see. It was a long scabbard of some sort ornately decorated in animals, fish, and birds. Jumping to the ground, I held it up to him. "Is this it please?"

"Yes mortal, the blade will not come out until you are within ten strides of the Norn. Now take off my arm ring and put it on your right arm only." Looking at his arm I saw a gold ring brace on top of which was a big pearl and four white ones, the big one jet black. "The pearls are enchanted to help you to survive underwater for some time, the black one will summon a water elemental of some kind."

"Summon a what elemental? You say some strange words Mr Tam Lin."

"A water elemental is a water spirit from the astral plane of water, a very powerful one."

"Oh I see I think."

"Do not think child but listen. You have to travel into the fire swamp to escape this realm child."

"If you call me child once more I'll scream."

"Scream away child." So I did. "Now if you have finished put the arm ring on your right arm now." So I twisted it on my arm and looked up to him. "It is too big." To my surprise the arm ring shrank to the right size of my arm, onto my jumper cuff. "Now you have the strength of ten men to help you to hold Caledfwich, and you only simply push down on to the pearls to get them to work."

"Do they stop me from drowning?"

"Yes."

WOW "Wicked!" I shout hands in the air.

"Yes, wicked. Now I have given you the rule of three: namely my essence, the sword and the ring of strength. I need you now to kiss my hand so I can rest." Ooh okay. So kissing his hand I stepped back. "Farewell mortal child, now I can sleep." As I looked at him, he was swallowed up into the tree and disappeared. "Good bye Tam Lin" I whispered.

\* \* \* \*

Now what do I do? I turned to the dark lake, the problem now was how to get back to the ledge, as I could not see it from here. Oh well, I would have to swim I supposed. So I waded up to my knees. I stopped. Hold on, I looked at Tam Lin's arm ring and the pearls he said would help me swim and not drown. So I put the scabbard down by the water and pushed down on one of the white pearls and stood by to see what would happen. I was completely covered in a blue halo of misty air. As I looked down at myself the blue halo was down to my socks, up to my head and even all round my skirt and hair. Oh wow this is crazy. So I waded in up to my waist and I could not feel the coldness of the water and holding my skirt I let it drop into the water to see if it got wet. It did. Oh I see you get wet but not cold. So in I dived into the dark water and began to swim under to see if it was working.

Hey it was as if there was no water in my mouth at all, I was not drowning at all! And with my hair and skirt flowing around me it was great not to be encumbered by wet clothes for once as the blue air gave me some buoyancy. Going back up to the surface I swam over to the island to pick up the scabbard and stood up to my socks in the water. Now how do I swim with the scabbard? Ah, I know, so I pushed my hair to one side and I put the scabbard down the back of my jumper into the waistband of my skirt and hoped it would stay. So with the scabbard on my back I splashed back in the water and into the crawl stroke. It was a bit difficult due to this big scabbard but I carried on and swam out into the darkness. As I came up to the other side I began to tread water and started listening for a waterfall noise. No, not here, so I swam on a bit more till I heard the faint sound of water in the distance, headed on to the distant sound and I soon saw the ledge where I swam up to the waterfall and tried to climb up, but it was impossible due to the flow. I had to swim to the ledge where I pulled the scabbard out of my jumper with my right hand and I threw it over the lip.

As I pulled my wet body out over the lip and stood up I could see my gear was still in one place, but the batteries of my torch had gone out. The blue halo around me gave me some light and then all of a sudden the entire halo dissipated and flowed out of me into a blue ball leaving my hair and uniform and my socks all dry and warm, then the ball rolled into the lake. Oh my, the weirdest things do happen to me, but it was a valuable lesson and one I must not forget. I sat down and felt around in the dark found my bag and I pulled out some glow sticks which I placed on top of dinghy so I could see all that I had to do this morning if it is morning, as I had lost track of all time down here. It was most strange I did not feel sleepy or thirsty or hungry at all. I pulled on a pair of black stockings over the socks, put my hair into a pony tail, straightened my tie and jumper and skirt, found my blazer and put it on even if though it was still a bit damp and put my baton inside my blazer and, with my damp shoes on, I then tied up the scabbard to the belt and my bag and I put it all into my dinghy. As I was about to go I noticed the bag of fish on the floor and the small knife...Hmm, ah, I put the knife in the side of the scabbard and then kicked the smelly bag of fish into the lake, but as I did it split open and all the fish fell out along with a small bottle and I quickly grabbed it before it rolled into the lake. Yeuk what a smell, so I put it in the water to clean it and washed my hands as well. I sat down by the dinghy and looked at it in the glow of the sticks on the dinghy and noticed it was all completely

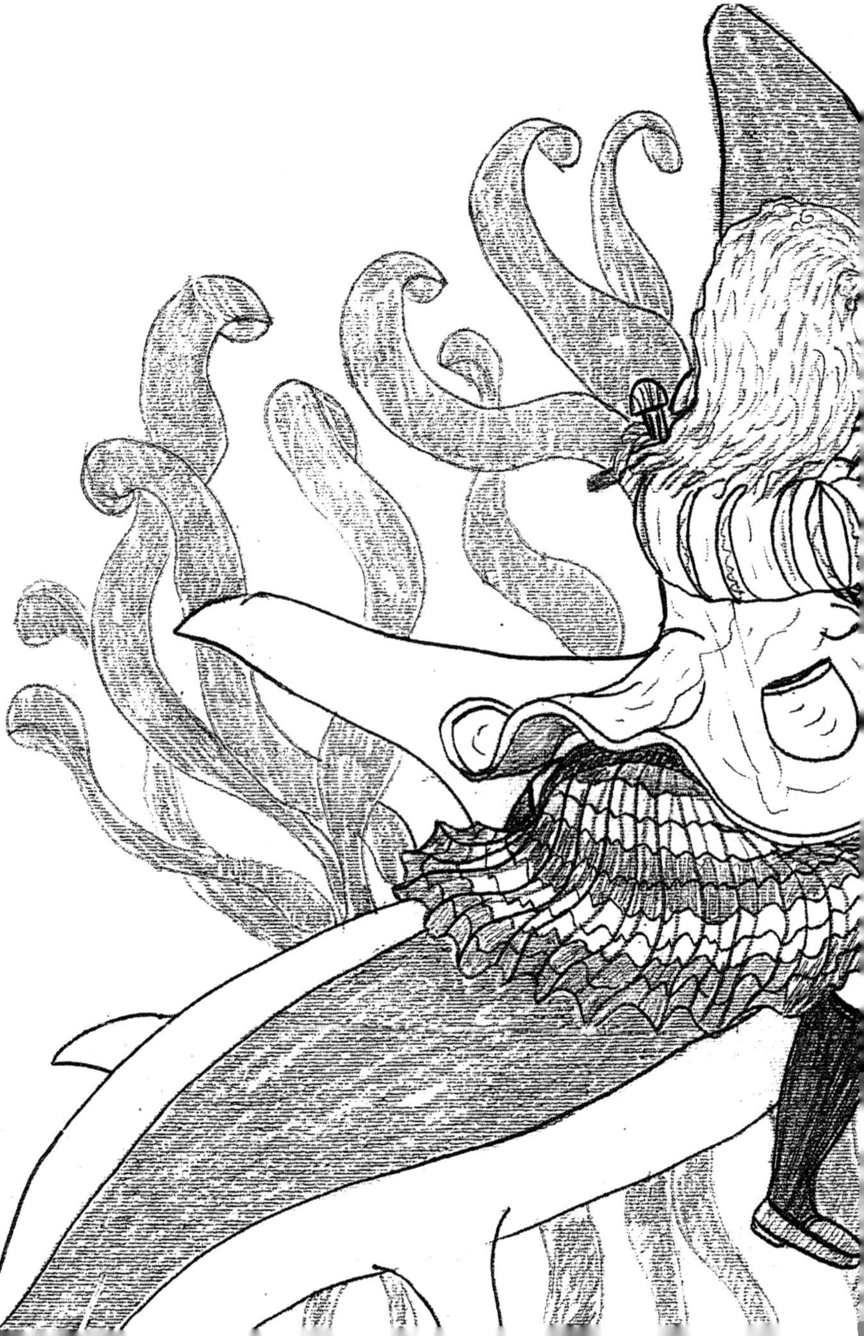

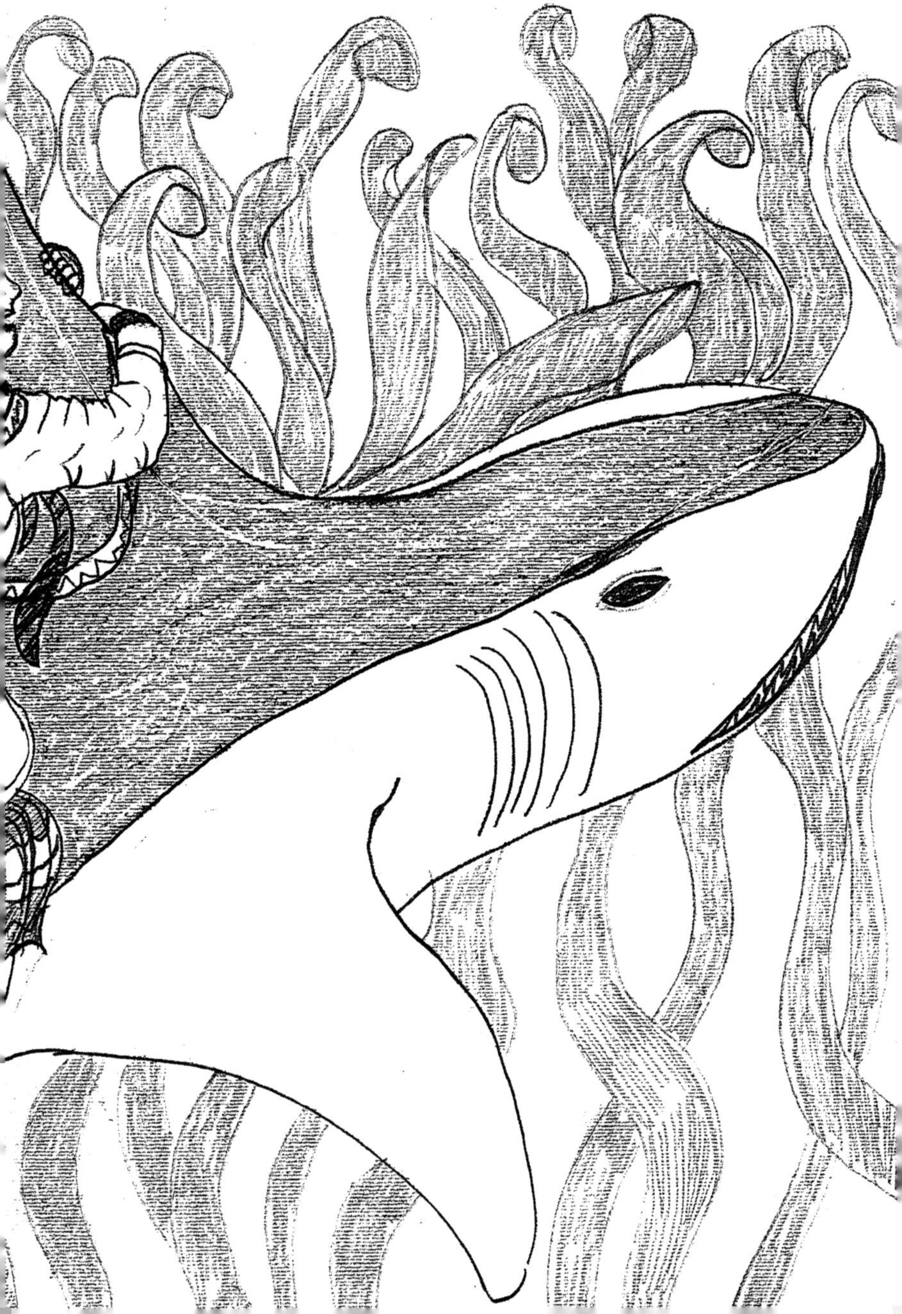

covered in some sort of signals, and it had a blue plug on top, and as I turned it round one side was clear and as I looked in "Eeek" I screamed as I dropped it into the dinghy in panic as inside was a face looking back at me.

"HELP ME YOU," a voice from inside the bottle cried in a very shrill voice. What in God's name is it now. "HEY YOU IN THE SCARLET JACKET CAN YOU LET ME OUT OF HERE?"

"Who are you?" I asked as I picked up the bottle. "LET ME OUT AND I WILL TELL YOU."

"What are you please?" I ask. "ME, WHO ARE YOU?"

"I asked first."

"I AM ELLA THE TROLL WITCH, VERY POWERFUL."

"If you are so powerful how is it that you are in a small bottle?"

"HA, LONG STORY MORTAL."

"Oh no, not you as well."

"WHAT DO YOU MEAN, AS WELL?"

"Mr. Tam Lin said it, he called me mortal lots of times."

"OH HIM." Do you know him? "YES, HE IS A LEGEND DOWN HERE."

"He is?"

"YES. HE WAS CAPTURED BY THE NORN AND TRAPPED IN A TREE. PLEASE LET ME OUT. I WILL GIVE YOU LOTS OF TREASURE."

"I do not want treasure. Can you tell me the way out of this hell hole please?"

"YES."

"I need to find the well of time and wyrd."

"DID TAM LIN SAY THE WAY TO THE WELL?"

"He did not say how, but it is the way to escape this place."

"AH, HE WOULD NOT, BUT ONE HAS TO THINK OF HOME AND REALM AND THROW ONESELF INTO IT, BUT THE NORN WILL NOT BE HAPPY, NOW LET ME OUT."

"No, you can see me to the well, then I will let you out."

"HO YOU MORTALS STRIKE A HARD BARGAIN. OH VERY WELL, I WILL SHOW YOU HOW TO FIND THE WAY TO THE WELL."

"Thank you, I think. Okay Miss Troll which way

"YOU HAVE TO GO BACK UP THIS TUNNEL INTO THE BIG WATER CAVE AND GO DOWN THE BIG MIDDLE TUNNEL ON INTO THE FIRE SWAMP."

"Why is it so named?" I asked. "HA, THERE ARE BROODS OF SERPENTS WHICH BLOW CLOUDS OF VENOM AT THE ROOTS OF YGGRDRASIL. BELOW US IS NIFLHEIM THE BOILING VIOLENT HVERGELMIR, THE THIRD ROOT OF THE WORLD ASH TREE. IT WAS IN THIS PLACE THE CRAZY OTTER GOD CUDBR AND ALL HIS CLAN WERE CAPTURED BY THE NORN."

"That does not tell me why it is named the fire swamp."

"OH DID I NOT SAY?"

"No."

"FIRE DEMONS, BIG ONES FROM MUSPELHEIM."

"Demons" I cry, my eyes wide. "YES FROM SURT'S REALM, ONE BIG NASTY FIRE GIANT. HE WILL BE AT RAGNAROK, THE DOOM OF THE GODS."

"But gods do not exist, there is only one God."

"REALLY, MORTAL LOOK ABOUT YOU. CAN YOU SEE ONE GOD'S WORK? YOU ARE AT THE BOTTOM OF THE MULTIVERSE OF THE NINE REALMS."

"Okay. I have heard too much and my poor head is splitting, I need a pill."

"NO NO." When I had put the bottle in my bag, I saw a box of paracetamol so I had one with sip of water. Now lets see I have got it all, yes. Right on with my life jacket, put my dinghy into the water and get in and I set of to my destiny.

\* \* \* \*

# Chapter - 5
## Day - 3

# The Caves

As I did not want to get my school uniform too wet again I laid on my back in the dinghy and pushed with my hands and legs on the walls until I reached the big water cave. I pushed off the last bit of wall into the flow of water from the waterfall and rolled over onto my front and thrust my hands over the side of the dinghy up to the cuffs of my blazer and, paddling like mad, I thrust the dinghy into the fast flow of this big opening and with only the lights of the glow lights on the dinghy shot into the darkness of the access to this wide tunnel. Shooting along nicely in the flow I pulled my hands in to warm up and I sat back up on my knees to see if anything which might be in front of me. Ah yes, green light some way off. As I glided nicely on my way I was wandering how my torch had gone out so fast when I was with Tam Lin, as the batteries were new, oh well it cannot be helped by wondering why. As I was nearly at the green lights I lay down and pulled my baton from inside my blazer in case of some unforeseen incident. But as I glided into a big cave all in green light I saw it was full of big mushrooms. "Oh my God look at them all" with my mouth wide open, all different big mushrooms. And that one at the back, now that is ridiculous, that one is as big as a house.

This cave was full of them, big ones and small ones, and I coursed meandering in and about the islands full of mushrooms and the smell was so, so incredible as I paddled on. Soon I was lost in a forest full of big fungi and toadstools, the water was all brackish in colour and I looked over the side to see my reflection in this water and had a big shock, my hair was now all fair not brown, my lovely brown hair had all vanished. I bet that was that bloody Tam Lin and his essence that he gave me, my mother's going to be so mad she liked my brown hair. Oh well, I'll have to get used to it. Now let's figure out a way out of here and so finding a bigger channel using my baton as a paddle I followed it for some time into the greenish light until I saw on a big island the most strange sight of a chariot - ah no, its a cart. Oh good heavens look at it, its huge with two big goats that were yoked to it as well. It was so beautifully carved with animals, birds, the sun and the moon all glowing green in the cave's light, so I pulled out the bottle and asked the troll witch inside what is it. There was a cry of panic from inside and she cried out "MOVE, MOVE THAT'S THE CART OF THOR, ODIN'S SON, HE MUST BE OUT HUNTING GIANTS."

"Who" I ask her? "THOR THE THUNDER GOD AND HIS HAMMER THE MIGHTY MJOLNIR, NOW PLEASE MOVE ON" she cried in a very small voice. "All right keep your hair on," and I put the bottle back in the bag. As I glided past the two goats just looked at me as if to say "What is it?" and I swear that they both then laughed at me. Drifting on past that strange cart all I could see was more big mushroom islands, so as I pushed on into the green. I saw a flicker of red light in the distance which appeared on my left hand side. Ah, is this it then? So pushing on the glare got very bright as the flames lit up an opening into a lake of flames, and drifting to the opening I give a good look in. Eeek, how am I going to get past this lot! The whole lake was on fire with burning vapour. Then the dinghy started to be dragged in and I tried to stop it but I burned my hands on the cave wall and then I was dragged in. A big flame shot over me and I ducked down into dinghy and then I felt a burning on my back "eeek" I cried, my lifejacket was on fire. I jumped up

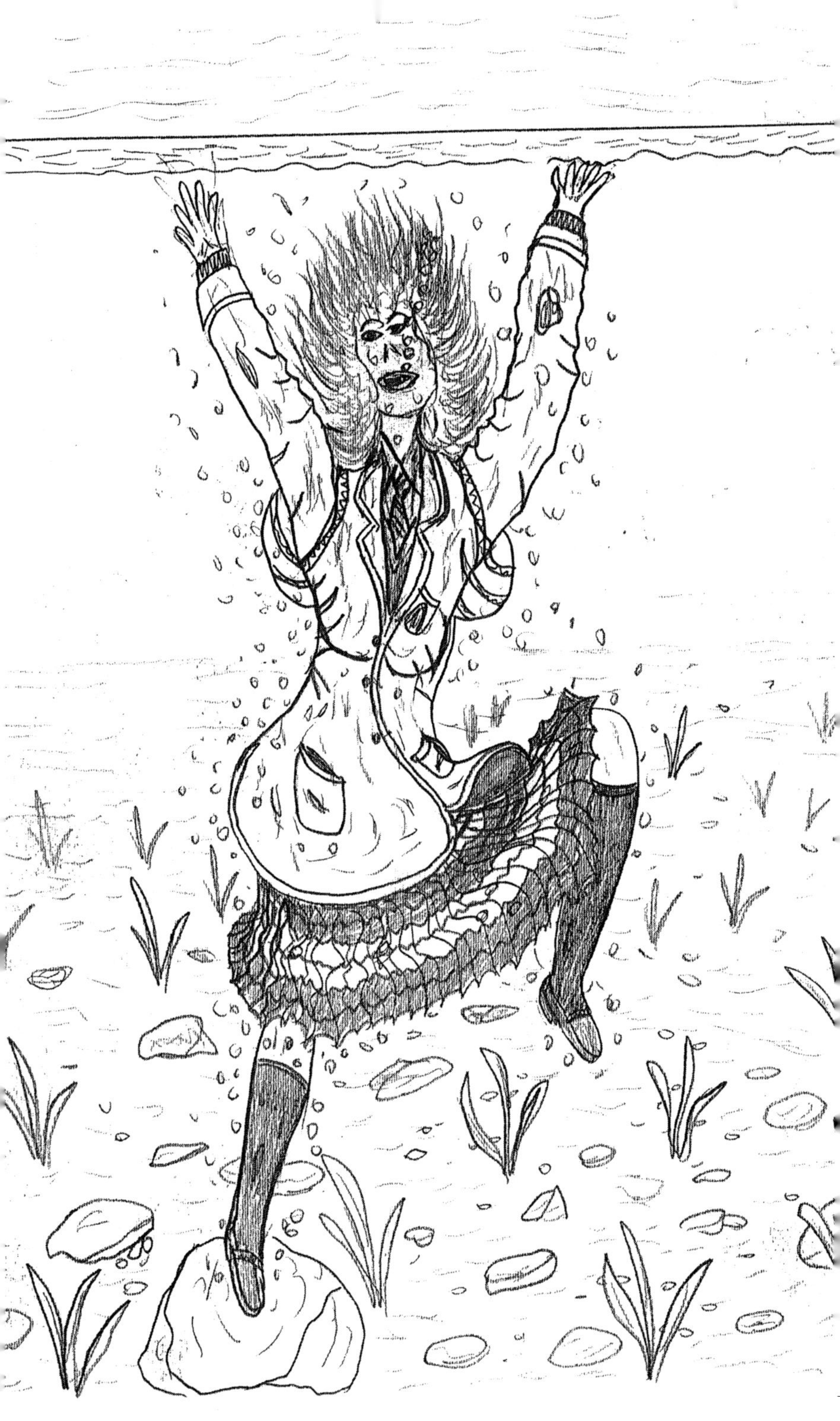

quickly to get it off but it was no good so I had no option but to roll over the side into the water where I had to rip of the now useless lifejacket and swim up behind the dinghy and I grabbed the back and began to tow it back into the cave of mushrooms to a nearby island where I dragged myself out and as I stood up the water all gushed out of my blazer and skirt and suddenly I realized I had just swum in my uniform again without thinking about it. Oh my God I am getting too good at it. As I pulled up the dinghy I saw it was untouched by the flames somehow, so I sat down in it wondering what to do about the lake of fire and I put my bag under my head, lay back and I fell asleep.

## Chapter - 6
### Day - 4

# Big Mushroom

I awoke to a voice yelling at me from my bag which I was using as my pillow "GET UP YOU MORTAL, YOU SCARLET LAY-A-BED." What? Where? How? "Hey" I shout. I have been asleep in my wet school clothes again and I rolled out of the dinghy with stiff arms and legs. Aaaahoo, God I need some warmth. I sat on the dinghy with my head in my hands I asked the troll how long I had been asleep. "TOO LONG.."

"How long?"

"SEVEN OR EIGHT HOURS OR MORE."

"Really that long?"

"YES." Good, and I got up and I was all clammy as I rolled over to the water to wash my hands and face, hey this water is nice and warm. Oh sod it, so I dived in head first into a bubble bath almost and I come up spluttering and gasping, Wow this water is too warm. I swam in the shallows where I sat and pulled off my shoes and lay in the warm water to warm myself up. As I lay I noticed that the water here was nice and clear with lots of bubbles rising to the surface so I pushed off to have a look about as I did my swimming exercises, and as I was about to get out I saw something big and round not too far under, so not even trying to dive down I let my wet and heavy uniform pull me under. As I sunk down I saw it was the top of a large mushroom sat on the bottom and I had an idea, a nice big wet mushroom which was almost as big as my dinghy, that will do nicely.

I swam back up and pulled myself out, off with my wet blazer and into my bag to find the fish hooks and line, and ran back into the water and dived down to the big mushroom, where I hooked all the lines on the sides and then back up for some air back down again and I grabbed all the lines and I jerked it up so I could swim under in order to use my right arm to push it to the surface. As I climbed out I pulled it out to have a good look at it. Yes this mushroom was just about the right size to cover the dinghy, so I managed to tip it over onto its back, this will do. So with the knife I had found on the otter I began to strip off the bottom to make it bigger. As I put the knife back into the scabbard it glowed all red. Wow that was strange, oh well. I pulled the dinghy over to try it for size. Mmm, not too bad with the dinghy mostly camouflaged. Oh my! I looked down at my uniform and I was all covered in brown filth and my stockings as well, so I pulled them off and my socks, and I had no choice but to wade back in to wash myself off. As I lay in the shallows after washing myself I wondered what to do with my bag as it was too heavy for what I had planned to do with the big mushroom. So I climbed out dripping wet but very warm to empty my bag of the things I no longer needed to keep. I sorted out the items I needed to keep and put them in the waterproof bag and I ate all the food I had left and drank all the water and then I dug a hole by a mushroom and put it all in and buried it all. Then I put my shoes and socks in the bag with my blazer, baton and the scabbard in the middle of dinghy and tied it all down.

As I picked up the bottle to put in my skirt pocket there was a voice from the troll. "HEY YOU SCARLET" cried the troll witch. "What do you want now?"

"LET ME OUT, YOU PROMISED."

"When did I say that?"

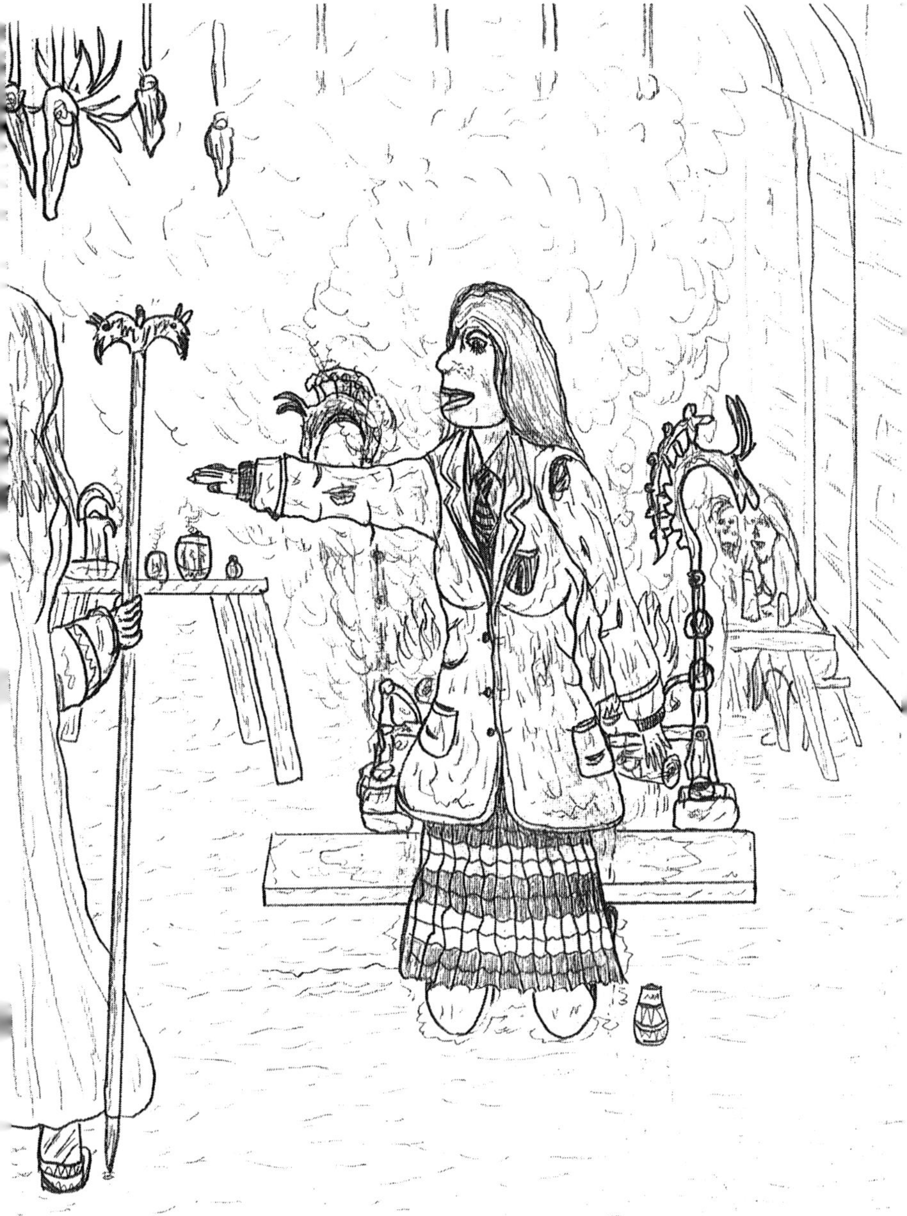

"SOME TIME AGO."

"No, you can tell me of the Norn please."

"YOU MEAN NORNS."

"No I said Norn."

"AND I SAID NORNS, THE THREE SISTERS TO NARFI THE GIANT OF THE NIGHT. THEY SIT BY THE ASGARDS ROOT TENDING THE WELL OF WYRD."

"Huh, but Tam Lin said Norn, not three of them."

"AH, HE MEANS THE OLD ONE WHO HAS GONE A BIT MAD."

"Huh, how mad is mad?" I ask. "MAD AS A BOX OF FROGS, AND I MEAN BIG ONES. KNOW THIS MORTAL SHE HAS BEEN ENCHANTING VERY POWERFUL VIRGINS FROM ALL TIME AND SPACE FROM ALL THE NINE REALMS AND MIDGARD TO TAKE THEIR ESSENCE AT THE WELL." Essence, that word again. "Tam Lin gave me his to stop the Norn."

"HE DID, DID HE?"

"Yes he did."

"WHY?"

"He said I was a powerful virgin, and I had to stop the Norn."

"HO HO HO, GOOD LUCK WITH THAT ISSUE."

"What do you mean by good luck?"

"HA HA, KNOW THIS MORTAL, THE NORN WILL BE

SURROUNDED BY ALL HER ENCHANTED MINIONS."

"What kind of minions?" I cry. "OH, LOTS OF OTTERS, MERMAIDS AND KEPLIES."

"Mermaids, otters , kelpies" I cry. "YES BIG ONES."

"Oh my God, please tell me this is not the truth?"

"WOULD I LIE TO YOU MORTAL?"

"Oh shut up you, let me think."

And I thought of what to do; I made holes in the top of the mushroom, pushed the fish hooks though the top and under the bottom and tied all the lines to the dinghy and stood back to see my work. Hopefully this wet mushroom top would keep the dinghy from too much harm. I sat down to put my last pair of stockings on which I had left out, put the bottle into my skirt pocket and pushed down on to one of the white pearls and I was all blue halo again as it appeared all around me, only two left now. I pushed my dinghy and the mushroom into the clear water, waded in and sunk down under it and swam to the front and turned on my back to see. Yes it was working! The mushroom's buoyancy was holding down the dinghy nicely, and I tied the lines round my chest, turned to the fire lake and began to swim under pulling the lot into the lake. I had to duck under to keep most of the mushroom and dinghy under water until only the top was showing and hopefully the surface of the wet mushroom would keep the dinghy safe from most of the heat. This swim was like a gigantic bubble bath, and looking about I could see that most of the flames were floating on top the surface. As I swam on I saw spinning up big corkscrews of whirling flame from the fiery furnace deep below me. I was happy to find that the blue halo also held back most of the heat as I swam in and out of the fiery columns. I dove down when necessary to avoid most of the flames on top as much as possible.

After an hour or more into this swim, I saw an opening up ahead, clear of flames or columns of flames, so swimming in that direction I surfaced to find myself in a large clear opening of water. I span about and I could see the top of the mushroom was badly scorched and bits were missing as well. I only hoped the dinghy was still in one piece as I turned back and swam on till I saw a large dark island where I could have a rest. While swimming on the surface I saw a very strange-looking tree with three green branches all thrust up into the air blowing green vapour up into darkness. I stopped swimming and I hung motionless to have a rest and I pulled out the bottle from my skirt pocket and held it up and I ask the troll inside "what is that?"

"YOU FOOL IT IS THE EVIL DEMONS I TOLD YOU ABOUT. THE BIG SERPENTS THERE ARE GNAW-FANG, GRVEE-WOLF AND ROOT-RIPPER. I had mistaken them for a tree and, oh my, I looked at the bottom and it was crawling with serpents. It was at this point one of them looked at me and I lost my pee again, as I do so hate serpents more then bones and skulls, and shaking in fear I dove down under to swim away very quickly, down into the depths towing the mushroom-dinghy load very, very fast - they say fear lends you wings - but in my case arm and leg work.

After some twenty minutes of swimming a dark well of black appeared in front of me but the blue halo lit up a big underwater tunnel. It was very dark and I wished I still had my torch with me as I was swimming blind. As I looked back the only light was from the fire lake and the glow lights on the dinghy, but the mushroom had gone and the dinghy had lots of bubbles in its wake, oh no the dinghy had sprung a leak. Oh well, not a lot I can do but swim on into this dark tunnel, and I was so grateful for the buoyancy and the light the blue halo gave me. As I swam on a light at the end of the tunnel appeared at last all in green and it was very bright and as I swam up to the surface I saw it was a vast cavern. The green light lit up a pattered maze on the roof of this big cavern, and it was very beautiful to look at. As I pushed my hair out of my eyes and looked around I saw a beach of white sand, so I dove down to poor old dinghy and pulled it up to the white beach. As I tried to get up onto this beach my feet sunk into the white sand and I fell backwards onto my bum with a crunch back into the water. Ahh, as I sat up I grasped a handful of this white sand to look at it. It was chalk, very crunchy white chalk. As I put it back down I saw my stockings were all shredded with lots of holes, oh my that was my last pair, so as I was still sat in the water I rolled them off and I pulled the dinghy to me to find my black school socks and shoes and put them on, but as I did I saw cracks on the bottom of my shoes. Oh no, these school shoes were new last term, mother's going to be so mad at me, but then shoes are not meant to be swum in nor is my school uniform for that matter. I stood up and pulled on my dripping wet blazer which is not easy to do as I put my arms into the arm holes I had to pull quite hard to put it on due to the wet arms and button it up, pull my hair out and straighten my skirt. And pulling on the lines I managed to pull up the dinghy onto the beach and once I was on the dry beach the blue halo disappeared again into a ball and rolled into the water and left me all dry and warm again.

"HEY YOU IN THE RED" shouted the troll in the bottle "LET ME OUT, YOU PROMISED."

"Oh in a minute" I said feeling the warmth of a dry uniform for once, how long will that last I wonder. I sat down and had a look at my dinghy. I could hear the hiss of escaping gas from somewhere so I took out of my bag the scabbard and put it down, untied my baton and all the lights on top of the dinghy, had a look into my bag for something to stop the leak, but it was not to be. So I lay on my back in my dinghy one last time, and I tried to think of how long I have been lost down here in this mad water world, and how I have had to swim out of trouble more times then I could dare to think. I lay dreaming of home and school for some time, my mother must be frantic with worry about me after all this time and my dad as well. And poor old dinghy gave one last hiss and lay as flat as a pancake. My faithful friend who saw me through so much pain and terror had gone, and I cried for some time over the loss. The last item I had with me now from the start of this adventure was my bag.

"HEY YOU SCARLET MORTAL STOP CRYING AND LET ME OUT. I HAVE SEEN YOU TO THE NORN'S CAVERN AS PROMISED NOW LET ME OUT."

"Oh all right I heard you." I sat up to dry my eyes, stood up and pulled out the bottle and I look into the face of the troll. "What do you call me scarlet for troll?"

"OH BECAUSE OF THE SHORT JACKET YOU WEAR."

"Oh you mean my school blazer, it's not scarlet. I call it burgundy."

"BURGUNDY! I NEVER HEARD OF IT. ALL RIGHT PINKIE-RED NOW LET ME OUT."

"Oh, all right hold on" and I pulled the blue top off, "here you go little troll and good bye" and I stood up.

"HAOOOW, HEEALL, FREE AT LAST, HA HA." With my

eyes wide open, oh my God, and I looked in terror as a cloud of grey issued from the bottle into a horrible big troll witch. EEEK as I fell backwards onto my bum I threw the bottle away from me. "NOW MORTAL YOU ARE MINE" and the troll grew into a monstrous green bald-headed and hairy-bodied mother troll with long big teeth and long wicked sharp claws. I crawled backwards, stood up and I ran for it, but this chalky sand was slowing me down, so I turned to the lake to do a header.

\* \* \* \*

And did I make it? NO. A big claw grasped the top of my blazer collar and I was lifted high into the air kicking and screaming. "NOW I WILL TAKE YOUR ESSENCE" cried the troll as she floated me high over the lake. "THE NORN CAN HAVE YOUR BODY" and she opened her mouth very wide. It was then I kicked her in the chin "God help me" I cried desperately. THEN a miracle happened as a beautiful bright light shone in her face and bedazzled her. A brilliant force issued from my school blazer's badge into the appearance of St. Diana. As the troll mother reeled back she shouted "YOU HAVE NO POWER IN THE NINE WORLDS SPIRIT, GET YOU GONE."

"You are wrong chaos spawn. I have power over all virgins who call on me who are in need of me and are in danger of evil intent, troll witch" and I watched this angel-like appearance of an athletic young woman in hunting garb with bow, spear and shield, but best of all was the sword of light and she thrust it into the troll witch who SCREAMED AND EXPLODED INTO GREY VAPOUR AND VANISHED. I was flung away into the air where I landed sideways in the lake, not the thing to do as I was in no shape to swim out and I sank like a stone into the dark waters.

# Chapter - 7
## Day - 4

# The Well of Wyrd

The next thing I knew I was lying on my back on the beach looking up at a dripping wet angel, not the thing you see every day, then I was horribly sick and I nearly burst my lungs with coughing up water. Then a voice said "Child you are most troublesome, three times I have helped you and now by the temple accord I cannot do so any more." I sat up to see this woman who was now in a long white Greek style dress now all dry and glowing all white. "Please how are you here?" I asked her as I patted my blazer's left hand side to see if the school badge had indeed gone, yes it had , oh my. "Know this child, I am the goddess Artemis of Ephesus, to you St Diana, the goddess of hunting and childbirth, virgins and chastity and you child have caused me lots of trouble in the last four of your days."

As she sat down next to me I looked at her in awe, my mouth hung open very wide, I then poked her in the side to see at I was not dreaming. "Child I am as real as you are, now shut your mouth and listen well, you have only one chance to defeat the Norn as you have on you the means to finish the task set by Tam Lin's queen Mab."

"But you said you are a goddess can you not do the task as I am only a child as you lot keep on telling me?"

"A child if only, we deities cannot interfere in mortal ways any more, if we did it would be like the old days again when the gods sent their avatars to live and influence mere mortals to do their bidding. Look at Troy for a start and the ten year war."

"But what happened to the troll? I did not see too much after I hit the water"

"Oh the sword has apparently sent her back to her home realm."

"Oh where is it now?" and I looked about for it. "Ahh, it has gone back to my twin."

"Mmmm who is your twin please?"

"Apollo, the sun god of light."

"But I have seen in books that Greek mythology was but a myth." She just smiled at me, "Ah yes the word myth is an old Greek word muthos for story and the word mythology- logit-study, who do you think taught man to read and speak child?"

"Oh I am so sorry I did not know, but why me please I am nobody special as I am only 14 and I am still at school and now I have got to stop this Norn somehow?"

"Because child we are here and nobody else, so know this child the Norn at this time is feeding on her last victim , she is Urd the eldest of the three sisters who has gone mad and who gazes into the past and spins the threads of fate of man and the gods and your fate as well child. So grow up child, you must be brave to face the Norn as you have the fey sword, the arm ring of strength and Tam Lin's essence in you to help you. But now I must be going for if Hela the goddess of death finds me here she would not be very happy with me."

"What the goddess of death?" I shouted. "Ahh. do not worry child she is probably trying to catch some hapless Viking man for his finger nails for that stupid ship of dead mans finger nails she is building for Ragnarok, the doom of the gods."

"Good" I said. "Now here is a vial of ambrosia for you."

"Huh, what Ambrosia rice?"

"No, stupid child, the food of the gods. Drink this down and you will be unstoppable for a hour or more. So now child I wish you all happiness in fate, choice and magic" and she vanished.

Ah bloody stupid gods, I wish they would not do that - it is so, so unnerving. I looked back down at my blazer to see the badge was back in place as good as new. Oh well no time like the present, so I might as well get ready, so I stood by the water and I pushed down on to the big black pearl to summon a water elemental, or water spirit and I hope it will not eat me. And not a thing happened (oh poo) then it went POP and up into the air it flew up into an arc over the lake (splash) and it disappeared. I hope it is not too big I thought as I stood by the waters edge to see what would happen. I saw some bubbles come up ...mmm.. THEN

\* \* \* \*

BANG a tremendously big creature appeared out of thin air and hit the water in a spectacular SPLASH. The wave of water sent me reeling back on to my bum back up the beach and I had to dig my nails into the white beach to stop me from being dragged into the lake as the water receded back again and, spluttering with water streaming from my eyes and hair, I stood up to see the most humongous shark I have ever seen in my life. "OH MY GOD" I shouted "oh no, have I got to ride that?" It was all black and white with one big dorsal fin. I jumped back in some shock as it rose up and looked at me with one big black eye as if to say "come on I have not got all day you know." I shout "have I got to ride you?" It then splashed its big tail once. "What, can you understand me?" One big tail splash. "Oh god, all right one for no, two for yes." Splash …. splash. Oh my, this is the most weird thing I have seen down here to date, all right hang on. Now what do I do? Ah yes, my flares - only two white and two red left now in a plastic bag, so I put them into the side pocket of my blazer ..mm.. ah I know as I took off the blazer and pick up the belt I got off the otter, tied the scabbard to it and I made a loop and tied it round my chest with the scabbard on my back, put back on my blazer and only did up the top and bottom buttons and left the middle one open. I pushed the belt loop though the gap in the blazer so I could put it over the dorsal fin, pushed my rounders baton inside my blazer, put my bag on my back and tried to pick that vial of ambrosia up and I put it in the top pocket of the blazer.

Oh well here I go as I kiss the dinghy goodbye and waded out up to my knees where I pushed down on to the white pearl, only one left now, and I was all blue halo again . "Mr. Shark are you going to eat me, yes or no?" It just looked at me, rose up and gave me a big smile full of big teeth as big as a cats and one big tail splash. "All right lets go" and I hooked up my school skirt and pulled myself onto its back, hooked the belt over the top fin and we were off.

\* \* \* \*

And it was all I could do to hold onto the fin as the shark took off at great speed on the surface and it was hard to keep my left hand still as it was apt to be hit by the spay and I waved it about as if I was on a parade. Then the shark, he or she, dived down into the depths, oh wow, and I began to shiver in some apprehension as to future events, and with my hair, tie and skirt flipping like mad around me I was so glad nobody could see my bare thighs as it would be so embarrassing for me, and now as the spay had gone I could at last grasp my left hand on the big top fin, and could look about me for anything to appear in this gloom of this dark water.

And as the shark ploughed its way on into the dark gloom it did not take long before some hideous looking creatures appeared ahead of me. The mother troll said something about kelpies and big otters but this looks like green weed beds but with the heads of women and horses and lots of long green arms all flowing about. It was then the mad shark shot into the weeds and bit one of the weed horses in two, and at this point I was no longer sat down but hanging on for grim death to the fin where I had to duck and weave to avoid all the weed arms that were in front of the shark. Then we were through them and then the shark rose up so quickly to the surface I had a hard time to stay on to its back and as we surfaced I saw land on my left side. The shark leaped up so fast I fell of its back as the belt loop slipped off the fin and I plummeted down its tail into the lake on my back, the shark then did a somersault onto its back and hit the water on my right side and the wave of water sent me flying on to the land, ouch. As the water ebbed way I sat up and I shouted at the shark, "you could have let me off you know you mad thing." It rose up it just looked at me with its big black eye and splashed its tail once more and dived down into the lake and disappeared. Stupid elemental.

As I stood up the blue halo rolled off me into a ball and rolled into the lake and I was all dry and warm again, right no more good manners from now on, I have got to get this job done. I took off my blazer, undid the belt and put the scabbard to the ground, then I straightened my skirt, tie and jumper and put on my blazer but left it open as I put the baton inside the blazer within easy reach. Now I have to look my best when I get home as I put on my bag on my back. I looked up to see this cavern was still all glowing green light and as I turn around I could see a big growth of mushrooms all glistening in the green light, oh my God more mushrooms, a whole forest of them, oh God not again.... then I heard a splash behind me and I looked back to see six heads of some mermaids all green hair and glistening tails who began to sing to me. "Ah ha, that will not work on me" I laugh as I put my hands on my hips, "you are funny." The mermaids all stopped singing and duck-dived down and pulled up wicked looking harpoons and throw them at me. S**t, I threw myself to the ground as the harpoons all just missed me by inches, and I jumped up grabbed the scabbard and ran for it to the mushroom forest to the cry of the nasty mermaids. As I glanced back I saw them crawling up the shore to the harpoons.

I ran into the mushrooms and tried to push my way forward into the canopy of fungi where I had to pull the small knife out of the scabbard to cut my way though. HUH and I pulled it out to see that it had got six inches longer then before. I looked at the scabbard in wonder, what is this scabbard doing to me I thought? Oh well. So hacking my way through into the forest the longer knife made short work of them until I hit onto a path. I looked both ways, this path had been cut though the mushroom forest and it was so quiet I saw nobody about at all up or down this path. I stood looking up and down and wondered which way to go till I looked up at the roof of this big cavern to see the patterned maze was glowing brighter on my left side, so choosing the left hand path I trotted up the path keeping an eye out for anything moving. It seemed ages before I heard the roar of lots of voices in the distance, so off the path into the cover of some very big mushrooms I went and scouted up as far as I dared to the edge of the mushroom forest. Oh my, just look at them all, hundreds of Shaggy all making the most hideous din I had ever heard and behind them was a small hill all glowing white with green lights flowing up into the air. The well at last, but how do I get past all the Shaggy? It was then that I sneezed very loudly and all the Shaggy looked at me.

Oh my God, and I pulled out of my blazer pocket the two white flares and pulled the tags and held them up BANG BANG up into the air they went all white over the Shaggy heads, who then screeched and yelled and yelped in terror. Right now for that vial of (what did St Diana call it?) ambrosia. I pulled it out of the top blazer pocket, broke the wax seal on top and I swallowed it all down. It was like liquid gold down my throat "AAEEE" I screeched as I fell to my hands and knees, and a very strange feeling overcame me as I started to glow all golden in colour and as stood up I saw the red mist of hate to all the Shaggy and I just ran into them all, yelling and screaming blue murder at them. Pandemonium broke out as all the Shaggy ran here and there and into them I ran clubbing left and right with the scabbard till I could see no more of them. Then I had to sit down and cool down for a bit, but not too long as I had to get up and go and see this Norn or die trying.

\* \* \* \*

Right now for the Norn and I began to run up the hill where I could see all round the well was white sand in piles which I had to climb over to get within twenty five paces of the Norn, and I could see a figure in the shadows her face hidden in a cloudy shawl and all round her lay the bodies of her past victims, and it made me so mad to see the carnage. At twenty paces away I saw her let go of her latest victim and I saw it was the girl in the silver catsuit I had seen some days ago, and as she fell to the ground I felt anger at the Norn. At nineteen paces the Norn pulled a golden thread out of the well and as she looked at me and gave a screech and an evil yell at me and I know that the golden thread was my fate. At eighteen paces she pulled out a golden half moon shaped sickle and she scored down my thread of my fate with the sickle. And at sixteen paces I felt great shocking pain all though my body and I screeched and I fell to my knees as waves of pain shot though me and I dropped the scabbard to the ground and rolled in agonized torment. And in my agony, to me came the vision of the death goddess Hela her face all blackness and half-flesh, her gaze is like a glacier on a frozen sea - all truth and terrible beauty, and she revealed to me the rotting hel-thing I would be if my courage failed me and I cried "NEVER." As I rolled up to my knees, I saw the Norn pluck my thread and I felt my heart stop beating and my left hand went to my chest, as it did my fingers bashed the top of my rounders baton inside my blazer and in one desperate left-handed throw I let it go and fell on to my face into the dirt. Then a thud, a shriek, something hit the ground and all the pain simply vanished.

I was up, grabbed the scabbard and ran the last six paces as I saw the Norn pick up the sickle and she turned to me as the scabbard spun out of my right hand and glowed all red and all the animals birds and the fish all glowed and began to spin in perfect harmony into a double helix into the shape of a glowing sword with very bright crystals all over the hilt and mountings and blade, then the scabbard just crumbled to the ground as did the belt and they turned into dust. There was a cry of "NO" as the sword flew with great speed into the Norn who shrieked and was thrown back with a terrible cry and into the arms of two more Norns who just appeared suddenly out of nowhere who clung to their sister and then all began to sing to me in rhyme and verse.

1. WEAVE AND SPIN LIFE'S THREADS BEGIN WHERE WILL THEY END WEAVE TWINE AND SPIN

2. ALL HAIL CHILD OUT OF TIME A RIDDLE A RHYME THREE PATHS LEAD FROM THREE REALMS

3. THE FIRST MOST SWIFT WENDS SAFELY TO YOUR HOME REALM THE SECOND TO THE QUEEN OF PAIN

4. THE THIRD PATH LEADS TO THE REALM OF AVALON TO THE ONCE AND FUTURE KING.

\* \* \* \*

As I beheld this sight in some disbelief and mistrust of the Norns rhyme all three glowed fainter and vanished out of sight. As I stood by the well the sword appeared in mid air and just hung point upright and by the light it cast I saw all the past victims of the Norn who were lying in heaps, all of them girls my age all in strange clothes some I recognized and some I did not. I crouched down by the girl in the catsuit and I closed her eyes, and I said a prayer for the poor souls who had the misfortune to be killed by the Norn for their very essence of youth. For some time I prayed on my knees, until I heard all the Shaggy all shrieking and crying and they were all coming up the hill towards me with murder in their black eyes. As I jumped up I pulled out my last set of red flares and I pulled the tapes and I turn to them and BANG BANG BANG off into the air they arched, as I turned and grabbed the sword out of the air and my knife–dagger (as it had now got longer) out of my blazer and with the sword in my right hand and dagger in my left hand ran to the well of wyrd.

The troll said to think of home as I stood on the realm of the well and held my dagger and the sword in an X above my head and I jumped into the well head first my eyes closed – "think of home, think of home," but there was no splash. Do not, do not, open your eyes. But I did open my eyes and as I did the light of the red flares lit up the name on the glowing sword in front of my eyes and as I read it, it was the word EXCALIBUR. Oh rats.

\* \* \* \*

## Chapter - 8
### Day - 5

# Dumnonia 450AD

Oh rats, I thought as I had jumped into green misty vapour. There was no splash but lots of vertigo, as I began tumbling very fast downward and I let go of the sword and the my now knife-dagger, and all I could see was green light but no water which was good by me so far. I was tumbling, "where am I going to end up now?" I thought and still tumbling head over heels all I could see was moving pictures of days gone by just like at the movies, but very spectacular. It was then I stopped tumbling and found myself in something of a very large bubble, or soap bubble, very transparent. But I was still moving too fast for me, then all the pictures all vanished into a cloudy blue colour and I felt the bubble stop and I could see green weeds and stones all in grey mud and blue water.

Oh no not again, as I quickly did up my blazer and took some deep breaths as the bubble popped and I was in freezing cold water (brr). I saw light above me as that bloody sword and knife-dagger landed in the mud right next to me, where I swam to a nearby stone and pushed off and swam up until my head hit something very hard, and I put my hands up to feel ICE. Ice, a whole sheet of it, oh my God, and I started to hit it with my fists but it was too thick to break up, then I started to sink down. Ah, the sword!, I thrust my legs to the ice and pushed off, I sunk to grasp the sword, then I pulled my back bag off as my feet sunk into the mud and I did a two-handed grab and pulled it out of the mud. As I turned to my right I saw some wooden posts not too far away so, half swimming, half walking and kicking up lots of mud I found a jetty of rough wooden posts in a line. It was then my air gave out, and in my panic I pulled back my blazer cuff and I push down on to the last air pearl and as I did there was air "aaaaahh" I cried as the water all glowed blue around me. WOW the effect was a bit strong and gasping air into me looked up to the ice. I thought I saw a dark shadow on top of the jetty and I pointed the sword up and thrust it up and it sliced through like hot butter into the ice, so I did a half moon cut, back down over a bit and did a thrust up again into another half moon and made a large hole to get out of this cold water. Then I bent my knees, and I thrust up into the middle bit of ice, but I overdid it as the ice scattered and my arms shot up into the air with the sword where my arms were grasped in a strong grip and I was bodily yanked out of the blue water.

\* \* \* \*

And as I hung in this grip I saw the biggest and the most hairiest man I have seen in my short life. He was in a bear cloak and just behind him was lots of snow fields all around and a lot of men and women all in cloaks and with horses and carts all loaded up with boxes. As my uniform and hair were still all wet and cold and dripping the intense cold hit me and I screeched and again I screeched in pain and suddenly I found myself being swung about. I let go of the sword and I flew over the ice, and I landed in a snow bank and lay as cold and desperate as I ever hope to be, but just before I blacked out a woman all in a green cloak with a gold ring on her head said to me "HELLO ANGEL" in old Welsh as I fell unconscious into a deep sleep. Then I was all wrapped up in a warm cloak and put on one of the carts, not that I knew of it at the time.

\* \* \* \*

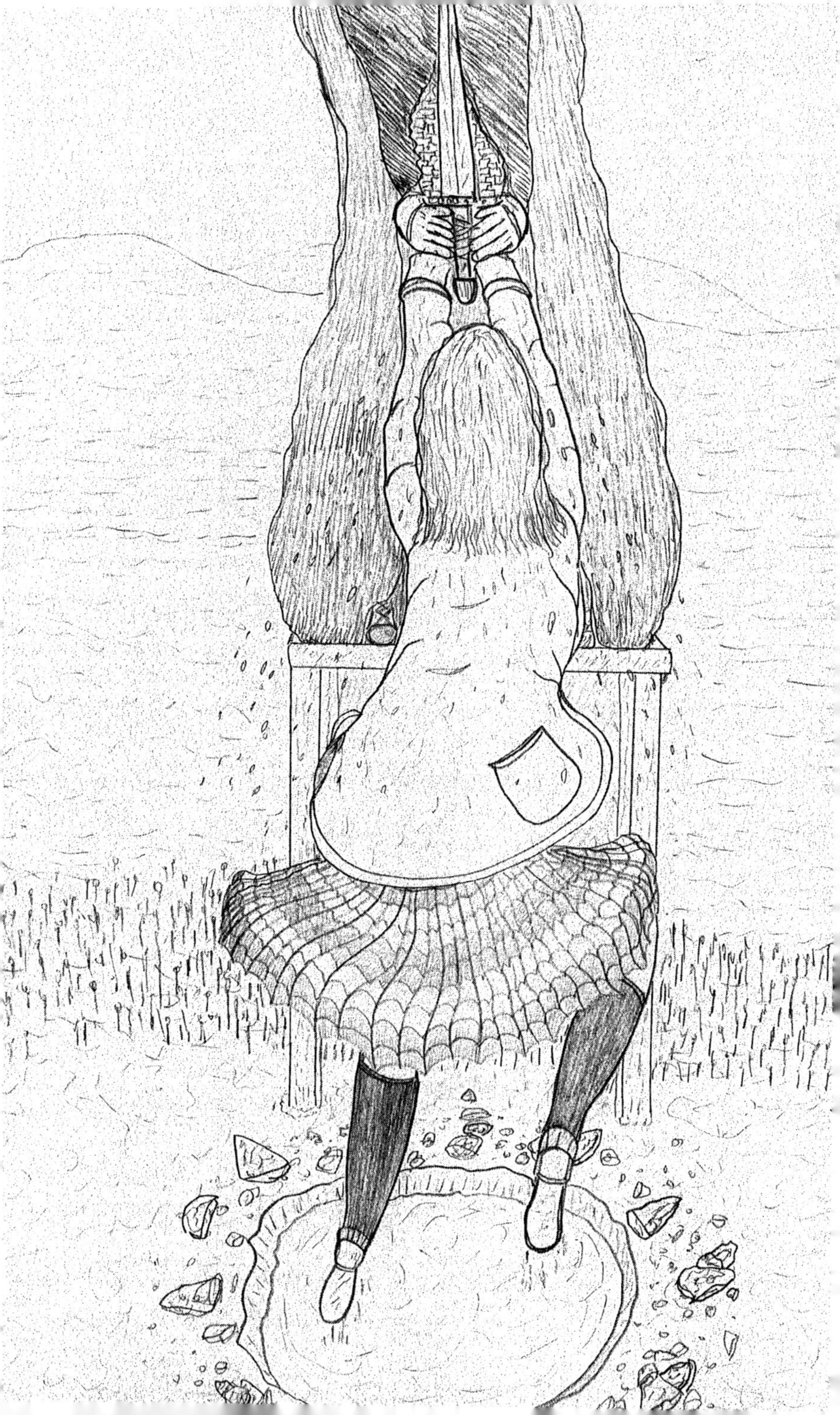

I awoke to the reeking smell of wood burning and the smell of unwashed bodies, and I floated in and out of consciousness. The next thing I heard was the babble of men and women and I could feel warmest on my right side, and as I opened my eyes I turned my head slowly to the right and saw a long fire pit and a high roof with lots of antlers on the walls and with strange looking things hung down from the roof on hooks, and as I turned my head to the left side I heard a gasp. As I opened my eyes wide I saw the woman in green who stood up and came to me and then she bowed low to me and gave me a wooden cup with handles with her head down. It was then that I saw the man who had pulled me out of the water. He had that sword on his knees and was sat in a big oak chair all carved with scrolls and floral ornaments by a table all carved in crosses and shields all with X and P on them, the symbols of Christianity, which was good to see. As I took the cup I asked her in modern English "where am I please?" The woman looked at me blank. So I sat up from the low bed I had been lying in, and as I swung my legs out I did a sat down bow to this woman in green, who then stood up shouted something to somebody at the side of the wall and a girl with fair hair who was dressed in rags ran up to her and fell to her knees in front of her. Then I noticed she had a copper ring on her neck and rags on her feet. The woman said something to her and she jumped up and ran to a door I had not noticed before. The woman in green then stood by the man in the chair, and the silence was so deafening behind me that I looked over my shoulder to see all the people I had heard, they were all looking at me and as one they all bowed to me. As I bowed back I thought "Oh very strange." I sat forward and looked down at myself. I was still all wet and sodden and clammy with clouds of steam blowing out of the back of my wet blazer. As I sat up I could see I was in a big looking long hall with a fire pit down the middle with what looked like hams hanging down over the fire pit.

It was then that the door opened and in ran the girl in rags to the woman, she fell to her knees and gave her a horn, which she blew and everybody in the hall stood up. I was still sat down and as I looked at the door a boy and a girl came into the hall and they were holding up an old man who was in old grey rags and cloak, the boy and girl wearing white robes with garlands of flowers and twigs all over their hair and all round the waists and cuffs and lots of red berries all over them. Now this old man I have seen in my books, the movies and plays all my life and been told stories of him by my grandmother when sat on her knees in my home in Swansea. As they got to me I saw an owl on one shoulder and a toad in his long white beard, and he had his eyes closed muttering to himself. They all bowed to the man and woman and they turned to me, and I said to this old man in modern English "you are Merlin the wizard aren't you?"

* * * *

The effect was both splendid and very frightening as all at once there was the magnificence light of essence all pink-blue which flowed out of me and into Merlin with lots of sprinkles and bangs out of my mouth. And as his eyes flew open the boy and the girl were thrown away to the side to many cries as the owl flew up to the roof, the toad jumped into the cup I was holding and standing in a spotless red robe with a black staff was a youthful version of himself. "Oh," he shouted, "I hate it when that happens to me," he shouted out in modern English. "You" he shouted at me as he looked as my dishevelled, ripped and water-stained rumpled school uniform, "You, you, what do you mean by appearing in nineteenth century clothes in the year 450AD, speak now or I will turn you into a toad."

"Twentieth century, actually 1970" I said "and Tam Lin said I had to jump into the well of time to escape the Norn's realm it was that stupid swords fault I got here in the first place" and I pointed at the man in the chair who held up the sword for all to see. "What, what, Excalibur. I never saw this" he cries . "You cannot be here in this time line girl, you must not" and he thrust his staff into my stomach pushing me back onto the bed, when then the woman in green intervened, and she shouted in Celtic something about a blue lake and the sword and the lady of the lake and she pointed at me and said something I did not understand to Merlin. "Well, well, well, it would seem the Duke his grace will have you as his mascot."

"But, but I was on my way home, I cannot be a mascot."

"Yes you can because you have on you the emblem of the great goddess and the colour of the emperor, purple the emblem of royalty, that deep red scarlet blazer you wear is the school colour is that not so?"

"Yes but."

"No buts girl, the Duke and his wife see you as a messenger of the old gods and an angel of the lord."

"What" I cried. "Right you, do not be so flippant and come with me."

And with that he grasped my school tie and he plucked me out of the bed, and he frog-marched me to the big door and out through the big leather curtain and out into the coldness of an overcast and gloomy winters day. My school shoes and socks sunk into cold mud and a bitter cold wind cut through my wet uniform and I shivered violently. Merlin saw me shiver, "Come on, you must get out of that wet school uniform, it stinks."

"Yes," I said, "I had to swim in it for some days" I said though chattering cold teeth, as I waded though the mud. "Please how is it can you speak modern English."

"Not now girl lets get you inside first." So trudging though the mud we came to a ramshackle hut where he let go of my tie, and muttering some words he raised his black staff and hit the hut and WOW a big white tent appeared in its place. "Ah, yes my yurt I had in 1262 - now we live in style." As he opened the door flap hot wind hit me in the face. Inside was fabulous and I stood with open mouth at the sight of bookcases, chairs, lots of china in chests and a clock all in glass and a big mirror – even a spinning wheel, stools and tables, but best of all was a bath next to a fire in the middle of his tent or yurt as he called it. He turned to me "You, off with all your wet clothes and shoes and have a hot bath, you can put all that wet uniform in that basket over there." So I did as he went off somewhere. I turned on the taps and hot water came shooting out with bubbles as well, oh boy, oh boy, and I stepped into wonderful luxury and I lay back (aaaaaa) so nice to my cold body. Merlin came back after some time and he handed me a cup of hot chocolate, and I looked in amazement at it. How, I ask, did you do this? "Ah ha, the look on your face was worth the magic. Oh my, that arm ring you have on your arm" and he took hold of it "this is of fey work. Who gave you this as it is priceless in this realm of man and world?" as he pulled it off my arm. "And if the barbarians in the hall had seen it you would not be here now as they would have pulled it off you and would have killed you for it." So I told him all about my last four days, the Norn and Tam Lin and St. Diana and the troll, and all that I had seen as I sipped the hot chocolate...."Mmmm, a good tale you spin girl. I will have to tell my teacher Blaise all about you, he likes a good tale now and then my girl."

"Please tell me how I got here and where I am"

"Allabury Hill Fort, girl by the river Lynher not too far from Bodmin moor as it will be called one day. And you my girl was pulled out of Dozmary Pool, a stone's throw from Jamaica Inn, there is a book about that." You mean to say that I am in Cornwall now? "Yes, my girl."

"But how do you know Jamaica Inn? You said that this was the year 450AD?"

"Oh did I not tell you? I live backwards in time. To me, sunset starts my day and at sunrise I go to my bed. Have you not read the 'Once and Future King' by T.H. White, and not seen The Sword in the Stone by Disney which I laughed all the way through? And now my girl I will give you one of the headdresses of the priestess of Avalon which you will need to get you home." Ah, the Norn said something about Avalon and the once and future king and that bloody sword's name was Excalibur. "Am I in King Arthur's time then and the round table and all his knights?" I asked him as my face lit up. "Ah, ho, ho, what have you been reading, too much romantic rubbish in books I see. No, there was a King Arthur, but the man who pulled you out of the pool, his name is Ambrosius, brother to Uther Pendragon and he is the source of all the tales of Arthur , and I know as I have written all of the books and the history."

"So this Ambrosius, what have I got to do for him?"

"Ah, he wants you to be his standard bearer. It is a great honour to you as you will be flying the Star Dragon Uther's battle flag."

\* \* \* \*

"But I want to go home" and I started to cry. "Now, now , girl do not cry I will get you home in time after the battle of Slaughter Bridge, but as I said you must wear the headdress and the cloak of a priestess of Avalon which is in Somerset in the summer county, so that I can get you to the holy well so that you can go home."

"Oh what" I cried "is it with all these bloody wells and water then."

"Ah my girl, water is timeless as it flows though all lands of time and space and is sacred to all. Now wash your hair and you can have this bone comb to do your long hair up as it did belong to the Angles and is now yours to keep. It is whale bone and has on it runes Aelgric made. The Duke captured some Angles and a boat last week and you will need it to look good for your journey to come." So as he got me a towel I washed my hair in the suds, he then held up this large warm towel in front of me. "Hey, I am naked" I said. "Do not worry girl I have seen many naked girls, so welcome to the dark ages." Not where I wanted to be, but wrapping myself up in the warm towel I got out. "Now off to bed with you, it is in the back and I will not need it for some time." So I followed him to the back where I found a large bed on the floor all in silk with lots of silken cushions of reds, blues and greens, all too comfortable looking for me. WOW was the only word for it. "All for me?" I asked him. "Yes and you can have this" and he pulled out from a chest a silk night-gown with lotus flowers and water lilies embroidered all around the neck and the arms. "For me ?" again I asked him as I pulled it over my head.

"Yes and you can also wear it under your school clothes as well to keep you warm on your way to Avalon. Now into bed with you, and the loo is at the back to the side of the yurt." So I pulled down this night-gown to my knees and began to make a nest of cushions and I lay down in my now warm nest and I wondered what to do next in this world as Merlin who was looking into some chests said goodnight and all the lights went out. As sleep took me, I thought of all the days in a very wet under world and my adventure to get out of it in one piece. My name is Angelina Janny Jones and this was my very fascinating story.

# The End

**Angelina Janny Jones will Return in Book 2 - The Ride To Avalon**